I0593979

THE CITY SCREAMS

AN ORDSHAW NOVEL

PHIL WILLIAMS

.

MMXIX

Cover design by P. Williams

ISBN-13: 978-0-9931808-8-0

Visit **www.phil-williams.co.uk** online for more information and
regular news regarding the writing of Phil Williams.
Join the newsletter to receive free content and be the first to hear
about new projects.

1

A pair of men stood either side of a doorway with an elderly resident between them, all staring at Tova. One was a triangle of over-exercised upper-body in a faded red bodywarmer, the other thin with a shiny green shell suit and the half-dark glasses of a serial killer. Tova had been getting suspicious looks all day, a young Westerner in Tokyo, weirdly *taller* than the locals, but these men were different. Their stares didn't accuse her of otherness – they said she was interrupting. Not the best welcome to her home for the next two weeks.

Tova mumbled an apology and hurried past, eyes on the carpet. She focused on the pattern: deeply faded yellow cross-hatched lines on a background of vomit-beige. A burnt patch by the skirting; a foot wide, that must've been some accident.

Reaching number 58, Tova shook the key in the lock, nervous, aware the men's eyes hadn't left her. Had she got the wrong door? The wrong key safe? The lock turned and she rushed into the apartment, closing the door immediately behind her. She shot a look out through the spyhole. The men were talking to the old woman now. They were leaning over her, and her arms were bunched close to her body. Did she look frightened?

Rubbing her eyes, Tova imagined Ethan grimacing smugly at this confirmation that one of Tokyo's dodgiest neighbourhoods was, indeed, populated by thugs. She shoved that thought away by imagining her best friend Ren's likely response: *Hey, Mr Shell Suit, how do you do? Quite well, indeed, let me tell you. I'm standing up to Granny at long last. We're not feeding your cats no more without pay.*

The combined exhaustion and excitement drew a smile to Tova's face. If the men weren't grumpily visiting a relative, there were a thousand other possibilities. So what. Tova had won an unlikely lottery for an impossible surgery, with a bonus opportunity to meet a celebrity, and she'd paid her own way to the Land of the Rising Sun to claim it. Alone. A couple of unwelcome looks weren't going to bring her down.

Tova crossed the room – tiny, with a single bed, kitchen bar, three-foot-wide bathroom partition – and took in the view. A wall of digital adverts flashed madly across the road: Japanese script, black on white, red, yellow, blue – a giant can of soda and a grinning young lady inviting you to BUY NOW! The image blinked and disappeared, replaced by a cartoon lion selling doughnuts. Eight storeys up, at the heart of a neon canyon, Tova appreciated the stillness of the room. She could practically see the air buffeted about by the crowds and cars below. Even between the taxi and the apartment entrance she'd been assaulted by wafts of garbage and stale cigarette smoke. This room had only the gentle tingle of an air-conditioning unit. The grim smells below replaced by the woodchip and straw of the soft, simple mats underfoot.

A quiet farm pen in a sea of ever-flowing trash.

Tova imagined the relentless noise below. Under the dazzling adverts, the colourfully dressed people were packed in tight. The din must've been why this place was so cheap. Not because gangsters roamed the halls. She'd made that case to Ethan herself, when he gave her the big-strong-boyfriend act about selling his car to come act as her bodyguard. Never mind that the old Volvo wouldn't cover fixing the blinking screen on his laptop, let alone a trip to Japan.

With his complaining face creeping to mind, Tova was glad Ethan wasn't there. Less so that Ren couldn't make it, but she wouldn't let that bring her down either. Now that she'd left all semblance of support back in Ordshaw, she could finally shut up the voice that scolded her for the hundred adventures she'd missed out on. Should've gone to university, should've gone travelling, anything but studying balance sheets in the Ripton Council offices. Now, she was finally living. Forget the grotty apartment – there was a life-size Godzilla poking over a building down the road, and in a matter of days Tova might be able to *hear* the surrounding madness.

Tova checked her phone, wanting to share that elated feeling. Still no messages. She'd had no signal since arriving. Mum would be waiting for her to check in, and the hospital would probably want to know she'd arrived safely. But until she connected to the Wi-Fi, she was *totally* alone. Her gut churned. The same thoughts had been swimming through her head during the flight. When Ren's job offer had come through, should she have refunded her own ticket, too? The surgery was a fantasy that wouldn't – couldn't – work. She was alone and wouldn't be able to buy food and would die shrivelled in an alleyway.

The lights across the street blinked again, the adverts bathing the room in a disco array.

The cartoon lion gave way to a familiar image. The giant face of Natalie Reid, the superstar from the estates of Ordshaw, *The Concrete Princess*. The woman Tova might meet, might actually *hear*, if Mogami Industries delivered on their promises. And Natalie had appeared right on time to say *The world's too small for you to ever be far from home.* With a little extra attitude from her moody expression: *And who cares, you're a trooper.*

Tova smiled back.

It was true, she was doing it, and had survived so far. The flight attendants had been unfaltering in their attention. She'd got through the airport to a taxi here without trouble. The surly driver might not have even realised she was deaf, since he lost interest in conversation once she showed him the apartment's address. And the city through the car windows looked infinitely cleaner and better organised than Ordshaw. This building, and those strange men, were nothing. The only real danger, the thing she was avoiding thinking about, was the surgery. Mogami Industries promised to achieve the impossible. It wasn't scary because it might fry her brain; it was terrifying to think it might work.

Ho hum.

In the street below, a wide man in a suit started gesticulating with short, sharp arm movements, arguing with an African in loose rags. Ren would've narrated this pantomime: *You sold me bad mojo – I told you it was only jam – take back your kitten!*

The big guy shoved the African hard. Tova found it difficult to maintain her uneasy smile as other pedestrians gave the men space. Would she be so calm if she could hear their shouts?

Once the goof was out of the room, Ki let himself in.

He thought she'd never leave, the way she repeatedly stopped to stare out of the window. But her stomach kept growling and eventually she overcame her indecision to creep back outside, giving him his chance to check out her things.

With the stories Ki had heard of Ordshaw, he'd hoped for someone more impressive, but *goof* was right. She was big, even for one of them – thick limbs, big nose, a whole train of black hair. And the clothes she'd pulled out of her bag were strange to say the least: shapeless trousers covered in checks, bright illustrated t-shirts (cartoon dragons on one), even a waistcoat. She'd gone out in an oversized sweater, bedazzled Converse and striped trousers. Not a lick of it matched. A patchwork girl.

Style wasn't a requirement, but her lack of it stung Ki nevertheless. He needed to leave her something nice. Make her pretty himself. As pretty as *they* could be, at least.

Standing on the kitchen bar, staring at the mess, he knew Mei would be furious at him for even considering it. He could hear her voice: Keep contact to the very minimum, the girl will do, however she looks. Don't take chances; this isn't Ordshaw.

Ki's eyes fixed on a pair of patterned socks hanging half out of the girl's bag. Blue and pink, thick cotton. He jumped off the counter. What did Mei know – he was here to make a bang, wasn't he?

2

"And how are you settling in?" Dr Eguchi asked, his exaggerated enunciation punctuated by a wider-than-necessary smile, both of which made it more difficult for Tova to read his lips. The intention was obvious enough anyway, from the condescending way he stooped over her. She smiled and nodded, as he said something about Kabukicho – not number one for most tourists. Ah ha. Ha.

He actually said the laugh, that was clear.

It hadn't been a great start, though he didn't seem to notice. Eguchi called himself the best ear surgeon in the world, but had a stilted, uncomfortable manner. The hospital was unwelcoming, sharing the same coldness Tova had experienced during her initial tests in Mogami Industries' Ordshaw office. No one met her eye, no one explained things in detail or took the time to see if she was comfortable. She got an impatient glare when she asked for the Wi-Fi code.

There was an air of coldness to it all, like the company resented Tova for winning their lottery. Tova Nokes: a contrary girl who wore bright clothing because she wasn't wealthy or important enough to be noticed otherwise. She could see their reluctance clearly enough in the way their lips curled with vague disgust. *Let's get this charity case out of the way so we can get back to our paying clients.*

The general attitude at Deaf Club was that Mogami were more interested in securing valuable patents than really helping anyone, and their prize was just a way to curry favour. Tova's family and Ren were behind her 100%, but Ethan had made his opinion clear enough before she'd entered the contest. "They're only giving it away so they can experiment on someone," Ethan signed. "And risking your body, to be like them, is disgusting."

He hadn't said anything when she got the confirmation letter, but his countenance changed. It strained his willpower not to make scathing remarks about Mogami's research, and to avoid joining in with the Deaf Club banter about it. Others were less subtle, laughing at her willingness to pay her own way over here, staying in a Kabukicho hovel, in exchange for pipe-dream surgery and a potential concert ticket. Ren stood up for her, though, insisting it was worth the airfare just for the opportunity to meet Natalie Reid, seldom seen in Ordshaw now she was famous. That was how Mogami had sold it, too. We won't cover your flight and accommodation, but we might be able to get you a meeting with a pop star; a showstopping way to celebrate Tova's restored hearing. They hadn't actually guaranteed the meeting, and it would probably come free anyway, as Natalie was one of these megastars known for Giving Back.

Eguchi moved around Tova and kept talking as she lost sight of his lips. She shifted to keep track but he turned her head – roughly – forward, a light shining on her face. Saying *please keep still*, maybe. Or maybe not bothering to explain.

The nurse, Hamada, watched from the side. Her expression was glass, partly hidden behind a paper mask. Though she was proficient in British Sign Language, which must've made her a rare asset for Mogami, she wasn't translating. The doctor had been peacocking for twenty minutes, reciting things Tova had already read about Mogami's research. There would be an incision, an implant and an injection. The state-of-the-art VHR-38 processor would come later. The operation combined an implant that amplified what futile capacity for hearing she had left with hormones that, by some miracle, could stimulate new cochlear hairs. The stuff of fairy tales, and a technique that would leave cochlear implant technology in the dust. It was completely unique to this hospital. Possibly because it was dangerous. The jokes in Deaf Club said they were experimenting with non-human hormones. But laughter aside, the Mogami website boasted dozens of success stories, albeit mostly Japanese children, possibly actors.

Eguchi stood in front of Tova again, his mouth moving, something about how long the surgery would take. She knew that too: a few hours under anaesthetic, a few hours under observation, then back home to rest for two days before they plugged in the VHR-38. If it worked, they'd repeat the process with the right ear.

If it worked. Tova was afraid to get her hopes up, but she tried to plan positively. Never mind the big dream of the concert and Natalie Reid; not far from her apartment was Shinjuku Gyoen, an oasis of parkland within the city. With even the barest hearing, she could listen to something approaching nature there. Birds, moving water, the rustling of leaves. Beautiful Sounds. She supposed. It had been fifteen years since she'd lost those experiences, and the memories had been supplanted by what she'd read in books.

Eguchi paraded back in front of her and waved a hand before her face to get her attention. He announced, clearer on his lips now he wasn't trying so hard, "I will see you on the operating table. Ah ha. Ha."

With a flourish of his lab coat, the Great Dr Eguchi marched out of the room.

Better a confident doctor than a likeable one, right?

Hamada (first name or second?), politely signed, "Be careful, at night."

Referring to Tova's neighbourhood again. Rubbing it in, that they were all a little bitter working with this pauper? What the hell, Tova told herself. She was going to own it. She signed, "It's lively, I like it there. And locals don't cause trouble with foreigners. Right?"

Hamada's eyes lightened, a little amused. She replied, "Not unless they want to."

Great.

"Are you ready?" the nurse signed.

Tova took a breath. She checked the clock on the wall. The UK was ten hours back, so it'd be coming on 2am at home. Her parents would be asleep, expecting news when they woke. Hopefully Ren was still up, not just Ethan.

TOVA: I've got about ten minutes, they said.

REN: And you're feeling?

TOVA: About as scared and mad as you'd expect.

REN: Well you're a damned hero and everyone would say the same. I'm having a party for you, sipping Bacardi and lemonade. On my own, seeing as it's a school night and that's Too Much for Ethan. He's rolling his eyes.

TOVA: What if he's right, and I'm taking a stupid risk?

REN: *Stupid* is taking anything he says seriously. The man's insisting on staying up nights while you're out there but won't drink, too? Come on. Wait till you can hear his voice, it'll be like a chicken being strangled.

TOVA: Oh Ren. I wish you were here.

REN: I am in spirit, believe that. We'll be here the whole time.

TOVA: You should sleep. But please don't.

REN: Relax, I'm going nowhere, still two days till production begins, and this is the way to spend that time. You'll be fine. Tova the Trooper. You pioneer it and next time we'll go out there together, for me. Did you see Godzilla yet?

TOVA: I actually did. And you know who else? Your princess.

REN: Oh hell. You ran into Natalie Reid!? Did Mogami deliver ahead of time? The show's not for five days!

TOVA: Wow, you're counting.

REN: You're not? So, tell me everything, spill!

TOVA: Ha. It's nothing. Just her face is all over the walls here.

REN: Rightly so. Have they at least given you your ticket?

TOVA: No, but it's why I'm here, isn't it? Not because I might hear again or anything.

REN: It's one to fulfil the other, Tova. You will be able to hear her. In person. In Tokyo. You know how special that is?

TOVA: If I can hear a toilet flush, that'll be special enough.

REN: You –

TOVA: They're here. Sorry. Some ten minutes. Speak to you when my ears work!

REN: Don't die!

Tova came around groggily, not sure where she was except that it was bright again. Everything in this country was bright. Pure white, this time. Oh – heaven? She *had* died on the operating table? Ha!

She twisted on the bed. Hamada came in wearing her paper mask, lips moving behind it. Was Tova supposed to be able to hear her? Had it gone wrong –

Tova's panic passed as Hamada held up an elegant plastic device. The sound processor, the VHR-38. Her thoughts clearing, Tova recalled she required a couple of days' rest before they would attach it. Quicker by weeks than the next best surgery, but an impossible amount of time to wait now.

Hamada placed the device aside, signing that it would be Tova's soon enough.

Eguchi entered lazily, performed a series of minor tests and gave a speech about his own success. Then she was sent away in a taxi. Back to stew in grimy Kabukicho.

Tova returned to her studio apartment and double-checked the stock of the supplies she'd gathered from the 7-Eleven last night. Enough for three days. Mostly egg sandwiches, and a few foodstuffs she'd convinced herself were *adventurous* with the least likelihood of unwanted bowel evacuation. There were triangular rice things wrapped in seaweed, milky-hued soft drinks and bags of what she hoped were potato crisps and not dried fish. Or – worse – banana.

She collapsed on the bed and distracted herself with her phone, fielding questions from Ren and Ethan. *Can you tune in to the radio now? Does it hurt? Do you think it worked?* Mum's platitudes were more one-sided: *Remember I love you my brave little girl!*

Little nothing. At the traffic lights, Tova could have used a Japanese man as an armrest.

Eventually, she abandoned the well-wishing in favour of Japanese TV. There was nothing but talk shows and something that looked like a family drama, instead of the violent cartoons and cruel game shows she'd expected. And besides, the subtitles were all in Japanese. Tova gave up to watch Netflix on her Samsung tablet. Enough adventuring for one day.

Ki watched her sleeping.

For all the fear and hatred they inspired, you couldn't deny her people looked harmless, especially at rest, like this. The fools in Mount Rishiri were wrong to fear them, with their old world mentalities.

Lying half-covered by a thin sheet, the girl had one leg hanging out of the bed. Her Western pyjamas, top and trousers, were a suit for children. The colourful pattern did her no favours. Were there *unicorns* on there?

As Ki studied her carefully, he steeled his determination. Someone like this, a little unusual, in need of guidance, was exactly why he was here. He studied her bandaged head, partly shaved on one side. Maybe she'd consider doing something different with her hair, now she was forced to. Her whole *thing* could change.

She had potential.

Ki could help her realise it. He was going to help all of them see the light, to hell with Mei's caution. How dangerous could interaction be?

*

Tova woke and blinked against the dark. She shifted onto her elbows, checking the deep shadows of the room. Nothing out of place, but an uneasy feeling nonetheless. When the VHR-38 was active, she wondered, would these night-time worries go away? The assurance of sound telling her there were no alarms, no distant screams, no stranger's footsteps in the room.

Who was she kidding. Sound would offer the opposite extreme, only making it harder to sleep. And she wouldn't wear the VHR at night, anyway. She *couldn't*, in case her big head flattened thousands of pounds' worth of Japanese technology.

Ruing the fact that she'd now stirred her brain into wakefulness, Tova watched the light under the door for shadows as people passed. No one there. Nothing wrong. The door was locked.

She found herself up, then, checking the door handle.

Dammit, this was Ethan coming through. *That neighbourhood's not safe. Those people are talking about us. Will you stop loving me when you can hear?* Give it a rest!

As Tova lay down again, she couldn't shake the feeling something was wrong.

Then it struck her – a subtle throb in her head – near her ear, like a vibration of sound. An actual sound? She sat bolt upright.

Nothing followed. Daft imagination playing –

It came again. A low, muffled thump, like the vibrations of a speaker. It came again. Not in her head, not a vibration – boom – she *heard* it. Again, a low, bass pulse. Again! It came in a succession of three beats, repeating. *Boom boom boom.* A gap. *Boom boom boom.*

She looked around quickly, unable to pinpoint where it was coming from. She wasn't supposed to hear anything without the VHR-38 clipped in, what was happening? She spun on the bed as the beat came again, quieter, then cut off.

A ring. High-pitched, chiming – where was it coming from?!

Then a voice. An actual voice. A man, speaking rapid Japanese. She couldn't make sense of the words – until they changed tone for something clearly enunciated. A letter and number, more important than the rest? *Key Zero.*

More rambling Japanese, the speech fading. Back into nothing.

Tova stared into the shadows, breathing deeply. She focused all her attention on her ear, trying to pick out something else in the abyss.

Nothing.

3

By morning, Tova was unsure if she'd imagined the sounds or not. She hadn't slept for what felt like hours, straining to listen, mind flashing on nonsensical thoughts, and finally woke in a numb stupor, unfocused. Jet lag, after-effects of the anaesthetic? She tried to shake herself out of it and wrote to her mother, *I think I heard something at night*, but even as she looked at those words, it seemed absurd. This was countless childhood nights repeated: the sleepless fantasies when her hearing was fading or after it was gone. Dreaming of it somehow coming back, that for a fleeting, waking moment she could hear again. Running to Mum before realising, in the pain of her parents' faces, that she couldn't hear her own shouts, even as she woke the whole street. It had been explained, many times, by different people, that post-lingual deafness could produce such dreams. Nightmares, really.

Was this the same thing?

Tova chose to take refuge in her tablet: nothing but Netflix and RPG apps.

The day passed dreamily, distantly. She didn't go out, not daring to navigate the city, and late in the day wrote consoling remarks to Ren about how well her new job would surely go. Ren would be a fantastic production assistant, and they would even give her a part in the movie when they realised she could Talk For England. Ethan, on the other hand, avoided discussing Tova's surgery in favour of dwelling on how much trouble he had finding a parking space in central Ordshaw. Maybe it was the jet lag, but Tova found her mind wandering to uncharted territory: is this my future husband? The rock who's been there since childhood, with so many shared experiences, the one that's Meant To Be. A pillar, with about as much personality as one. As Ethan droned on with additional complaints, Tova decided she didn't need to feel guilty about cutting him off so she could go to sleep early. She hadn't, she realised, told anyone about her night-time fears.

The second night of recovery came and went without

disturbance, but the thought of that little bass pulse and those words resurfaced in Tova's mind when she returned to the hospital. Rested and eager for the finale of the surgery, Tova dared consider, again: what if it had been real? After Eguchi did some introductory checks and wandered away, Tova signed to Hamada: "Can I hear anything without the processor?"

Hamada shook her head and signed back, "Your new hairs might be active, but the external processor is necessary to activate the implant. You'll be exactly as before, without it."

The nurse had mistaken Tova's concern for a fear of not being able to turn the sounds off again. The answer still counted, though. They'd supposedly produced new hairs in her inner ear, but these were not like natural hairs. They weren't strong enough to pick up sounds without the technology in the implant and processor. There was no way she'd heard those things at night.

Eguchi returned, beaming proudly. Tova's bandages were removed and she tapped the tender stitches, hair buzzed around them. Looking like Frankenstein's monster?

Hamada took the VHR-38 and signed, "I will activate it now."

Tova nodded eagerly.

Forget the midnight blip, this was real. She was a modern Columbus, conquering a new world – Tova Nokes of 12 Ripton High Street. Secretary of Second Thursday Deaf Club and all round soundless superstar, taking one giant leap –

Her head was pushed sideways as the VHR-38 clicked into place.

A muffled sound – the patter of unclear speech.

Tova jumped in her seat, a loose hand scattering things from the table. There was a whine, a high-pitched buzz, all around her. And something beyond it, a sudden plethora of noises, *clattering*. Nothing crystal clear, but all definably *something*.

Hamada adjusted a control and the muffled speech came again. Clearer. Actual words.

"Ms Nokes? Can you hear me now?"

"Yes," Eguchi said, "it is working."

Though fuzzy, his voice was as smug as his face had suggested it would be.

And by hell it was *glorious*. Tova echoed, with wonder, "It works."

For the first time in fifteen years, she heard her own voice.

Low, imperfect, but beautifully her own. Her eyes shimmered with tears. As she tried to say something else, the words caught in her throat. She heard her own gargle. She heard the tap of footsteps on tiles nearby. She heard Hamada's light, encouraging laugh and Eguchi speaking: "Now, we tune it. It will only get better."

Tova couldn't reply, but nodded, eagerly.

Tova lay awake staring at the line of kaleidoscopic colour that intersected the ceiling down the middle, coming from a crack in the curtains. She'd spent the afternoon with a grin that stretched her face to aching. She had taken a taxi back to avoid the full onslaught of Tokyo, to ease herself in, as Hamada had advised. Little steps at a time, though she'd had one or two fully immersed moments at busy crossroads. Outside the car, she'd heard the beep of pedestrian crossings, the honking of horns. The shouting of market vendors and the barking of dogs. Too many sounds to pick them all out at once.

She would walk tomorrow, to Shinjuku Gyoen. In a few days, when Mogami arranged it, she'd hear Natalie Reid live in concert. Spectacular things were coming.

But she hadn't dared use the phone yet, telling her family and Ren she still needed to recover. Though Ren had been joking about Ethan, Tova was genuinely nervous about what everyone sounded like. Ren's enthusiastic speeches would sound like pure spoken joy, wouldn't they? Would Ethan's reluctant monosyllables sound as dreary as they looked? His one-word responses to her messages said it was *good* her ear worked and that *maybe* they would talk tomorrow. She sensed his fear and she was afraid herself. The Japanese voices were unreal – the music chiming from digital adverts *insane* – but they were the detached sounds of this other world. Assigning sound to *her* world was terrifying. She wasn't even ready to unmute her tablet.

Lying awake with the VHR-38 in, Tova listened to the electric hum that surrounded the building, with pedestrians' shouts interspersed with vehicle engines. Distant muddles of music. Occasional noises coming from a room below her, indecipherable but unquestionably human.

She should sleep, to experience this properly once rested. But everything sounded so alive.

A new noise started above her head. A deep, rhythmic beat – low, heavy bass. Someone listening to a tune right above her head. *Music*, with the texture of sound, not just a felt rhythm. The beat was familiar – three repeating thumps. Exactly what she'd imagined two nights before. Tova frowned. It couldn't have been real before – not without the VHR-38 installed.

It became quickly clearer. Loud, like it was in the room with her. And the bass was strong – perhaps something she could have felt before. Was that it? They'd played it loud enough that she'd felt the vibrations, and semi-consciously mistaken that for sound. Possibly...

She relaxed, to enjoy it *properly* now.

Bass, my old friend. We're going to enjoy each other's company more than ever.

Tova awoke to someone talking.

Japanese words, nothing she could understand.

Right there – by her ear –

She spun off the bed, searching the shadows, as the chatter continued.

The speech was somehow impossible to pinpoint, but sounded close. The room was empty, definitely empty. Her eyes rested on the bedside table. The VHR-38 glistened blue in a glint of light from outside. It wasn't attached, there shouldn't be any sound –

The voice clearly pronounced a word she understood: "Ordshaw." Then it continued in rapid Japanese, before fading slowly away.

Hell. This was stranger than picking up a random sound. Why would anyone in this dive of a building be talking about Ordshaw? That couldn't be coincidence.

The voice was gone, leaving only cold, empty nothingness.

Tova whipped up the VHR-38, clipped it in and flipped the switch. It crackled horrifically in her ear and she half-tumbled out of the bed as she tore the processor off again.

Holy hell.

For a split second, a grotesque mix of white noise and something else – an organic, pained screech. It was right there – a noise right by her ear. But there was nothing. Nothing else in the room, just the dark.

She was too shaken to try the processor again, and suddenly

felt a long, long way from home. Shaking, Tova put the VHR-38 down.

She looked at her phone, light blinking to say she had new messages. The clock on her phone read 4:16. They'd be awake back home. But talking to them would make it real, and that sound was *not* real. There were no sounds that horrible.

Tova crept back under the cover.

Night-time fears, nothing more. Imagining it. It would be fine in the morning.

Everything would be fine.

4

Tova woke up calm, before resting her eyes on the VHR-38. The anxiety returned. She sat up, frowning, checking there was sunlight through the crack in the curtains. She was rested now, properly awake. Time to dispel those imagined horrors of the night.

She clicked the VHR-38 into place and carefully flicked its tiny switch, exhaling and listening for the sound of her own breath. No unholy crackle, this time. She breathed in, brow knotting further.

There was no crackle – no screeching – and no other sound either.

She breathed out, feeling the vibrations, knowing she was breathing, unable to hear it.

She clicked the device off and then on again.

Silence. Nothing at all.

She flicked the switch again. Again. Still nothing. Why?

She grabbed her tablet and played a video from Netflix, turned the sound to full, held it by her ear. *Nothing.* She scrambled to the window, threw open the curtains and looked down into the street, eyes boring into the bustle, willing its din to reach her. She'd had it yesterday. She'd had everything, the whole world – where was it now?

Tova leapt for her phone and brought up Dr Eguchi's number. She dialled and pressed the phone to her ear, desperate to hear it ringing. Not even a distant buzz. She held the phone away to check when it was answered, then spoke quickly, "I can't hear! I can't hear a thing – it's on and I'm listening, and I'm trying, but it's gone! Why, what should I do! Help me!"

She had no idea if the doctor replied, or was even there. It might have gone to voicemail. She hung up and took deep, calming breaths.

It *had* worked. There must be an explanation. Maybe they'd given her a dud battery. She spent half her life checking batteries to ensure she didn't miss devices' vibrations – it had to be that.

The phone buzzed, a text from Eguchi: *Do not panic. Come to the hospital immediately*.

Don't panic, fuck – when were instructions ending *immediately* ever calming?

Tova whipped on the first clothes at hand, threw the VHR into her day bag, and raced to leave, paranoia mounting. All her hopes – stupid, *stupid*. Something thumped overhead as her hand found the door handle. Not a vibration, a sound.

She froze.

It came again: a bass thump. Then again. She looked at the ceiling. That same music. Her mouth fixed halfway between elation and confusion. But it was *only* that music, not the sounds from outside, no ambient noise. She rapped a knuckle against the door and didn't hear *that*. She focused hard and the beat came again. *Boom boom boom*. A pause. *Boom boom boom*. Slightly quieter. Fading.

No! – she was losing it.

Tova threw the door open and ran for the stairwell. She bounded up the steps and charged along the hall of the floor above. She stopped at the apartment above hers.

Nothing, again.

The sound was gone.

Tova screamed, bent double, fists clenched. Loud, feeling her lungs shaking against her chest. The defiance of childhood supermarket trips – railing against a teenage party when everyone looked so damn happy – her not hearing a thing.

The door to number 68 opened and a middle-aged Japanese businessman leapt out, ready to hit something. His tie was half-undone and his face was puffy, like he'd been up all night. They both froze, locking eyes. Tova made a false start, then forced the words out, "Were – were you listening to music?"

The man scowled back, not understanding.

Tova pointed at her ear to explain through gesture, and the movement set the man off. His mouth worked quickly, his confusion replaced by taut-fingered, crooked-armed fury. Berating her in language she wouldn't understand even if she could hear. He pointed sharply away. Get the hell out of my hallway.

Tova backed off with her hands up. Now he'd started, the anger swelled in him. He followed her into the hall, one fist balling and his neck veins pulsing. Tova turned and fled.

*

Eguchi wasn't saying anything. He didn't need to; with his multitude of tests and tweaks, and still no sound in Tova's ear, his expression said it all. The experiment had failed. The operation, he insisted, could not have gone better, but her brain had rejected the new hairs.

"*After* I started hearing?" Tova signed uncertainly.

The doctor looked angry at her for undoing all his hard work, and she felt a stab of shame. Was it her fault? Had she done something wrong? Used the VHR for too long on the first outing? They had said nothing about time limits, nothing about risks to the technology. The only caveat had been that the injected hormones would take time to fully develop the hearing.

Eguchi left the room and Hamada signed, "Sometimes it is a difficult transition."

Tova gave an expression that demanded more.

"The device works perfectly," Hamada signed. "None of the components appear faulty. The tests yesterday showed your brain responding in the correct ways, your body too."

"And today?" Tova signed back.

Hamada hesitated. "We would need to do more tests to fully understand. If you are certain. You know, it can take months, years, to get used to hearing."

If you are certain? They thought she was lying? Or delusional, simply unable to cope? Tova replied levelly, the words coming out in speech at the same time as she signed, "I know sounds. I heard them until I was seven. I know what I heard yesterday, I know I can't hear today."

Hamada gave her a sceptical look. Of course, it had to be *Tova's* fault. She was the invalid, the idiot who couldn't even hear – *they* had done everything right and she had done something wrong. She couldn't let them twist this around. She thought of the words before she said them. *I heard something.* I definitely heard something. In her indignation, a speech then came without thought: "I heard something before the VHR was plugged in. In my flat. And last night – I heard words, clearly. *Ordshaw*, they said. Before –" She brought up the memory. "*Key zero.* A man's voice said that. *Key zero.* I heard those things, and I *know* I wasn't supposed to. Last night, something else. Something worse – horrible. What did you do to me?"

Hamada didn't seem to follow.

"I heard it!" Tova raised her voice. "You can't say there's nothing wrong – hearing something without the VHR plugged in – that's not supposed to happen, there *must* be something wrong."

Hamada shook her head, pityingly. Didn't believe a word of it. She signed, "It doesn't work that way. We'll run more tests to see what's happened. There are many settings we can trial – and if that fails, yes, we can do a brain scan. Please be patient. Do not give up."

Tova pointed to the empty doorway and signed an angry response: "It looked like *he* just gave up."

Hamada remained bunched up, ashamed, as Tova's eyes demanded a better solution. She'd travelled half the world, *alone*, spent all her savings, kept this secret from half her friends. All the while suppressing both the hope that this would work and the fear that Mogami Industries were doing something unstable. She had *heard* things. This was crueller than never having tried.

"Come back tomorrow," Hamada signed. "Rest. We'll do everything we can."

"Another operation?" Tova signed back. "Another injection?"

Again, Hamada didn't respond. Of course, there was no other operation.

Everything they could do would be nothing at all.

Ki looked up from his work, hunched by the vast weaving machine, half as wide again as his adjacent desk of computer monitors. The material was coming out smoothly, perfectly, and he didn't like to take breaks mid-job, but the girl's movement on the screens told him something was wrong. He spun his chair to face the monitors as she thumped onto the edge of the bed. Shoulders shuddering.

Bad news.

He turned up the audio.

She sounded like a wounded animal, blubbing with decreasing control. She had gone out wearing the pantaloons and waistcoat of an impoverished circus entertainer – was it any wonder she'd got in trouble? Had someone robbed the hapless tourist?

As her volume rose, Ki switched the audio off. The whine escalated through the floor, anyway. She was making enough noise to shake the floorboards, making someone above stomp and shout, cursing her. That drunk hypocrite; he blared classical music like it was punk rock.

Tova's cries didn't falter; she didn't even look up. She slumped further and buried her face in her hands. She hadn't reacted to the man's shouts. She couldn't hear herself, could she?

Ki pulled a mini-laptop over and brought up the hospital's login page. He checked her file. The latest reports were brief, but telling: *...claims she cannot hear, despite tests showing proper functioning. As with case DN43 – rejection of neurological interaction.* She'd swept in grinning like an idiot the night before. Ki had been planning to make contact today and her welcome gift was all but ready. He dialled Mei and spoke without introduction, "She's lost it."

"Huh?" Mei replied drowsily.

"Wake up, Mei, I need your full focus here. It didn't *take*."

"What?"

"The girl, it didn't take and she's drowning in tears. More broken than before."

Mei yawned loudly, hardly invested in the conversation. "Fine. We'll extract, try another angle, another time. Nothing lost."

"Nothing lost?" Ki hissed back. It had taken him months to set this up – he'd produced his very finest work, on a scale never before seen in Rishiri, or anywhere the yōsei dwelt. To say nothing of the effort he'd put in setting up shop in this rathole, close to this goof. "We're not done."

The girl stopped crying. Ki frowned at her suddenly thoughtful expression.

"Ki," Mei said. "They *will* catch up to you."

"No, we go with the backup plan," Ki replied defiantly. Tova was completely still, bar her eyes shifting from side to side, something having caught her attention. This was good, if a little weird. Not a total mental breakdown.

"If she can't hear –" Mei said.

"She doesn't need to hear, Ms Reid will understand. We'll put it in writing." Ki affected his best British accent, switching to English. *"The surgery failed but she still wants to meet you."*

"That's –"

"Hello?" Tova's voice rose up through the floor, a shout from below. On his monitor Ki watched her sit upright. Eyes wide – somewhere between hope and fear. "Who's there?"

"What's going on?" Mei asked.

"I don't know," Ki answered. "She's getting –"

"I can hear you!" She was on her feet, sounding desperate. "Please – you speak English?"

The man in the room above yelled again, thumping on the floor, and Tova took a few steps aside, like she heard that. Ki kept silent.

"What the hell is going on?" Mei said.

"Gotta go," Ki replied with a quick whisper and ended the call.

"Please!" Tova repeated, turning on the spot, searching the corners of the room. The man above kept yelling, but Tova didn't react this time, shouting, "You said something! Where did you go!"

Ki kept watching, hand tapping against the hilt of the curved blade propped at his side.

Interesting.

5

ETHAN: I'm checking the flights. I don't care what it costs, we'll get you back ASAP.

TOVA: I know it's late there, but how about you actually read my messages? I heard something, Ethan. Before the VHR was activated, after it stopped working. Someone nearby, talking about me. Distinct words, *key zero*, Ordshaw – *the surgery failed*. I'm freaking out.

ETHAN: I know! You never should've gone there alone, why do you think I'm up now? Come home.

TOVA: Look – if you want to do something, contact Mogami in Ordshaw. Whenever they open. Get someone to explain *exactly* what they injected me with.

...

TOVA: Well?

ETHAN: What will they say?

TOVA: I don't know – that's the point!

ETHAN: I'll wake up your parents.

TOVA: Ethan! At least pretend you believe me! Get in touch with people from Mogami's other operations, see if these words I heard could be connected or something!

ETHAN: Words like *key zero*? That's nonsense, Tova. You're just looking for something to blame.

TOVA: What? What's that supposed to mean?

ETHAN: I mean. We all knew it was a shot in the dark. Maybe it's best we leave it?

TOVA: The operation worked, Ethan. There's something else going on.

ETHAN: I'm just saying. How do we know for sure if you actually heard these things?

TOVA: Are you fucking serious?

ETHAN: You had a thirteen-hour flight, an operation, you're in a new country. The operation went bad. Yeah, there's something else going on – but I'm not sure it's anything suspicious.

TOVA: Go to fucking bed, Ethan.
–TOVA HAS DISCONNECTED–

Tova wished it was Ren who was keeping a night-time vigil instead of Ethan the Naysayer. She was wide awake and that voice had spoken in English. Not just that, he'd stopped talking when she shouted. She sensed, for sure, the man was above her. If not the businessman who'd chased her away from number 68, maybe someone else in his apartment, or one of the neighbours. She considered going back up, knocking door to door, but didn't know what she'd say.

It had jarred her out of her sorrow. Eguchi's operation was a disaster, but she wasn't going to sit wallowing with this weirdness to explain. Standing at the window, she watched the world in motion, searching for inspiration.

Her flight home was in ten days. Was there anywhere she could go beside knocking on random apartments or relying on the hospital? Were Eguchi and Hamada even to be trusted? They'd been certain everything was working properly yesterday; surely they could see what was wrong today. Were they hiding something? But Mogami were the only people in the world running these operations. The VHR-38 was their patent, the hormonal compound their guarded secret. Who else could she go to?

A car swerved up onto the pavement below, its sudden stop drawing Tova's attention. A big man got out, shoulders squared aggressively, beat-up bodywarmer familiar. Tova watched as the other door opened, the thin man in a shell suit climbing out. The pair from the corridor, the day she'd arrived.

The muscular one looked up, his face stonily focused, and immediately picked out her window. Tova stepped back with a gasp. He saw her. He looked directly at her – *for* her.

Why? What the shit, why?

Tova caught her breath for a second. She was being ridiculous. Paranoid now she was hearing things, or not hearing things – what a fucking muddle. *Something else going on with her surgery* did not extend to *random dangers around her apartment block*. She leant forward, venturing another look. The shell suit one was running full pelt for the building – his friend was already gone.

Fuck – they'd seen her duck out of the way and were racing up to get her. Whatever the reason, whoever they were – nothing was right about this and she shouldn't be here.

Tova grabbed her day bag and chucked in her wallet, passport and phone. She was at the lift before she realised they'd be coming up in it. She ran for the stairs instead, and got one flight down, heart pounding, before slowing to question her actions. They could be visiting a mother – on an urgent call – hell, maybe they *were* gangsters, but coming for someone else – why should they be here for her? Why would anyone want to hurt her?

She leant on the banister. Maybe she –

Something moved below: a door, at the bottom of the stairwell, flying open with such force it hit something and bounced back. It swung open again and the arm of the muscly man flapped past it, pushing in. He entered alone.

They'd separated to cover both exit routes.

Tova dropped out of sight.

They were here for her. They had to be. Was it them she'd heard talking? Not above her, but through a radio? Was her apartment bugged? After she'd seen whatever was going on with that old lady? Bloody hell bloody hell.

She glanced over the banister again: Muscles was bounding up the stairs, full speed.

Tova went down another flight, quickly, hugging the wall to avoid being seen, and she crept through the nearest door. A hallway identical to hers, nothing but entrances to flats. She gently closed the door, begging it not to squeak, and ducked to the side. She pressed herself against the wall and held her breath.

A shadow passed the crack under the door. There and gone in an instant.

She exhaled.

Tova waited a few moments more, then carefully pushed the door back in. She peered out, no sign of movement. She crept to the banister and looked up. He was gone. If they didn't realise she'd left, she might have some time while they tried to break in to number 58. Or they might start checking every floor.

To hell with it, she had to go.

Stumbling down the stairs, Tova ran as fast as she could. At the bottom, she hesitated briefly before leaving the stairwell and crossing the empty entrance hall. The lift counter said 8 – her floor. Tova rushed into the busy street. The next building down had a big set of open doors, the nearest cover. She entered to a long corridor of arcade machines. Dazzling lights flashed from all directions, rows of serious-faced men sat on stools pulling levers. Tova squeezed between them; the machines seemed to go on and on. Please lead somewhere, let there be another exit.

With a glance back over her shoulder, no sign of anyone following, she reached the end of the machines and found a doorway, sure enough. A man walked in, unlit cigarette hanging from his mouth. She ran past, out onto another street, vaguely aware of arms flapping behind her. People might've been shouting – to hell with them. As she joined a new crowd, keeping her head down, she finally took stock.

Had she really tuned in to a gangster's conversation?

6

Sitting on the grass, Tova hiked her knees up to her chin, trying to distance herself from the panic. She wanted to tell herself she'd overreacted – but she couldn't shake the idea that those men were there for her. They had picked out her window, run into the building and split up to block the exits. All after she'd responded to that conversation. That wasn't nothing.

The voice – the voice had mentioned Ordshaw. Said in English, *the surgery failed*. Was she being targeted for abduction? The sex trade might prefer a deaf girl; randy men thought it made you an easier pull.

Tova checked her phone. Still no signal. Her network didn't get on with the Japanese ones *at all*. She needed to jump on a café's Wi-Fi, but it was scarcely past 1pm, so no one would be awake back home anyway, not now she'd driven Ethan off. And he wouldn't be back for half a day. She could go to the police or the British Embassy – she had a whole list of addresses in her notebook – but what would she say. Between the businessman yesterday, and Eguchi and Hamada's frostiness, she wasn't enthusiastic about relying on strangers. The only other option was Ali, a contact in the Shinjuku Deaf Club who she'd messaged from home. A stranger at the end of an address. *Hi, you invited me to visit your club but did you know I'm also on the run after being lobotomised into hearing bad things?*

No. She'd call home, that's all. When they got up, when she got her head straight.

Tova held her eyes closed, counting slowly from ten to one. Eight, seven, six...at six years old she'd known terror worse, and earlier, than most people – witnessing the first approach of infinite silence. If she could survive that, she could handle a foreign city.

Though she hadn't exactly done much to *survive* her hearing loss, other than soldier through bouts of despair. That was safe, and never optional. She was never far from friends or family; her single long-term relationship was with a guy even less adventurous than her. Her mediocre job enacting other people's dull dull dull ideas was the exact opposite of responsibility. She barely walked to the pub alone. When had she ever fended for herself? What was she doing in Japan? What could she handle besides shitting bricks?

Start again.

Ten, nine, eight...

Take in the fresh air, the tranquillity of those smooth cropped hedges, let out the worries.

She heard a Japanese voice.

Tova snapped her head to the side, eyes open, fixed on a distant tree. This pocket of the park was isolated, shielded by trees. Definitely no one around. The towering Tokyo high-rises were hidden behind branches and leaves. But the voice came again – distant, but familiar. The male voice from the apartment. His tone changed as he muttered something – surprised?

Tova didn't dare speak. It hadn't helped last time.

"You hear me?" the man asked in Japanese-accented English. Louder, clearer.

There was *no one* here. Had the hearing implant actually fried her brain?

"You do hear me, yes?" the voice came again. Well-spoken, educated. He muttered in Japanese, then went quiet again.

Tova stood up hastily, scanning every gap in the branches. A skyscraper was visible through the trees, a long way off and mostly obscured. There was no way anyone could see her. A movement in the branches drew her eye; something small and dark, settling. A tiny bird she couldn't quite focus on at this distance. Was stress ruining her eyesight, too? Perfect.

As she turned on the spot, the voice didn't come back.

She scratched her temple where the stitches stood like bumps, flashing on cochlear implant horror stories they'd told each other as kids. Luka Bristow, a boy in Hanton, Ordshaw, had had an implant go wrong; it rewired his brain and shattered his sense of identity. His ability to feel pain was destroyed, making him an unstoppable killer, and he spent his life hunting the hearing for revenge. A bogeyman born of an attempt to be *normal*, an ugly and dangerous aspiration.

Except that story was *bullshit*, made up by either Tova or Ren themselves – take your pick. Luka Bristow came from Ordshaw,

London, Paris, wherever mattered most to your audience. An urban legend. Cochlear implants didn't touch the brain, and had as much chance of causing mutant accidents as a knee op.

But then, Mogami weren't exactly performing anything like cochlear implants, were they?

People at Deaf Club were half-serious when they joked about the company's research.

Tova's temple throbbed as something rang. A bell, of sorts. Chiming, again, again. She recognised it: the same ring as she heard in the night. A phone? The voice returned with a few quick words in Japanese before he said, "Now? You hear me?"

Tova stiffened. She slowly nodded.

"*Kuso*," the man exclaimed, some kind of curse. He spoke in Japanese again, one word clear: *HiWave*. Another voice tried to speak over him as he translated his conclusion: "It's the HiWave you can hear. Nothing but my voice, yes?"

He went quiet, waiting, and Tova heard his breath, like he was right next to her. But true enough, she heard nothing else. Feeling the nerves balling in her chest, she slowly nodded again.

"You're hearing a phone call. That's how we are connected, understand? Maybe you hear Mei, too? Say something, Mei."

"Something," his companion said, an icy female voice.

"You hear my lovely assistant?"

Tova nodded more enthusiastically. Her ear worked. It bloody worked. She wiped her face messily with her sleeve. She had to say something – to answer back. "Who are you?"

Her own voice made no noise.

"You're hearing my call," the man said. "I can't hear *you*. But I see you."

Tova focused on the visible sliver of skyscraper. To be watching from there he'd need a telescope and a very speeific vantage point. But there was nowhere else. Again, her eyes went to the tiny dark shape of the bird, still on its branch.

"You can't see me," the man said.

Tova tensed. She took a step to the side, another, edging towards the path. This voice had come before the men, after all...had she not escaped at all?

"You're safe," the man assured. "I want to talk. To help you."

The woman on the line exhaled irritation. The man ignored her.

"Let's start with introductions, *Best of Friends.*" He said the phrase as though quoting a TV show. "You'll feel better if you know who I am? My name is Daiki. Ki for short."

"Ki," Tova repeated the end of his name. Pronounced *key*. Flashing on those two words she'd heard – *Key Zero?* "Ki." Unable to hear herself, she said it louder.

The man responded, apparently watching. "Ah, you like it? A common name."

Tova had no idea if it was, so said nothing.

"I have a question." He cleared his throat and made a few shuffling noises as though checking through notes. "Ah. Yes. Do you like cheese?"

Tova knotted her brow.

"Cheese, you know? Because I think you are *grate*."

Tova's frown deepened. What the hell was going on?

"Grate. Spelt G - R - A - T - E. Because, cheese, yes?"

Tova remained absolutely still.

"I think you get it. No? Okay – perhaps you like cats? Cats are magical creatures, no? You look like a cat person."

Tova shook her head, only recalling allergic coughing fits at her Uncle Larry's.

"I ask because" – Ki slowed down, to get this right – "I am *feline* a connection."

"What..." Tova mouthed at the absurdity of this exchange.

"Ah so bright!" Ki exclaimed, more enthusiastically. "Sorry – a ray of sunlight – no. Wait. I think it was your smile?"

Tova raised a hand to cover her mouth; she didn't feel like she was smiling, but just in case. His voice was so vibrant, cheerful – breaking the dark cloud that had hung over her all morning.

"You majestic woman," Ki said triumphantly. "You are in good health and humour. I am honoured to make your acquaintance, honoured that you can hear me."

Tova's mind raced to work out how this was possible – where this voice had come from. She'd heard him in the apartment, got away, alone, and he was somehow here? No way she could pair this joker with the angry businessman. She signed, *Who are you? What's going on?*

"That is adorable," the man said. "My English is proficient, but I do not know your hand language, sorry. We can use a yes/no system. Yes?"

Tova hesitated, but gave a slight nod.

"Excellent. Now, I have a confession to make and you will think I am a creep. I was not going to talk to you, but those men forced my hand. Will you please forgive me?"

She didn't dare move, in case this whole illusion shattered.

"So. I know who you are." As Tova's face fixed in alarm, Ki hurried on. "I saw you arrive, and I was curious about this most majestic woman. I learnt why you were here, in our beautiful city. I thought, when I discovered your situation, to offer you a gift, for the successful operation. To share your joy. Your name is Tova Nokes, correct?"

What in hell...

"You come from England's most notorious Ordshaw. Gangster city?"

Tova gave Ordshaw's reputation a blank look. Ki laughed.

"No, not everyone in Ordshaw is a gangster. Not everyone in Tokyo is a comic-reading pervert, either. You come from somewhere very normal, I suppose."

"Normal." Tova mouthed the word, always reserved for other people. Often insulting.

"But *you* are special. Only, I saw what happened. Those men – those terrible men. Well done for escaping them, you did very well. And forgive me please, again, for following you here."

Tova searched the trees again, focusing on that dark blur of the bird for want of anything else to pierce with her gaze. She demanded, internally, *How did you follow me? Where are you?*

Ki sighed deeply. "I am so sorry you have seen this side of our city. Do you know who those men were?"

Tova shook her head.

"You have not seen them before?"

She hesitated. Whoever he was, whatever this was, he at least sounded innocent of involvement with those thugs. She nodded.

"You have? In the building?"

Nod.

Mei cursed in Japanese, and Ki's tone as he continued suggested he was thinking out loud, not addressing her directly. "I do not think they were ordinary Kabukicho criminals. I saw them – they went straight for the room. Do you have any idea why that would be?"

Tova was still. Now he posed the question, the thought that they came because she'd heard his call seemed ridiculous. They might have been coming anyway, having seen her before, a white girl here for the picking. Why shouldn't they be ordinary criminals?

After she hadn't responded, Ki continued, "Tova, you can only hear me, correct?"

Tova nodded.

"The HiWave is very advanced. Exquisite sound. Top quality connection. No ordinary wireless." Ki's proud explanation was interrupted by Mei, who railed off something quickly in Japanese, seeming to scold him. He verbally batted her off. "Ah ah, it's nothing. We are having a conversation here. Tova? Your hearing is connecting you to a most experimental piece of hardware. It is a headset, like headphones, but unlike anything in your stores. A circumstance like that might draw particular attention."

A circumstance like that? Tova gaped. Randomly hearing a stranger's expensive headphones was supposed to encourage thugs to break down her door? She signed her confusion: *What are you talking about?*

Ki continued, "We can help you. Mei, we can protect her, can't we? Tell her, we are the very best."

"We are the very best," Mei said, dryly, then added something in Japanese.

"Please, in English," Ki replied. "Mei suggests we leave you alone. I don't want to scare you, or interfere with your holiday, *please* believe that. But I saw you in trouble. I cannot in good conscience ignore that."

Holiday – that made Tova laugh. Not in a good way.

Ki continued, "So what shall we do? The first question, I suppose, is where to go."

Tova bit her lip, fingers fidgeting with her pocket, wanting to sign: that wasn't the first question on her mind. Forget going anywhere, she needed to know what was happening to her. Without the VHR-38 connected, there was no way she should be able to hear at all. Her hand went up to her scar. The VHR-38 had stopped working on the night when she'd heard the voices. Had his HiWave played a part in the malfunction – could it reactivate the processing unit? It was still in her bag from her trip to the doctor; she dug it out.

"Are you –" Ki started, but she waved her free hand for quiet.

She explained, vocally, not caring that he could not hear, "If I can hear one voice, maybe it can still work. Maybe there's still a chance."

She clipped the processor in. Please, let this work, give me –

Tova's ear crackled with white noise, such a sharp, loud sound that she winced and dropped to a knee. As she grabbed at the volume control, other sounds cut through so fiercely that her hand seized up. A scream, high, strangled – angry.

Another scream, from a different direction, so loud that Tova went rigid. Another – more – joining in a horrific chorus. She twisted, trying to source these sounds – howling apparitions, close, and getting louder, closer – a hundred voices screeching, tearing at her, like people charging from the trees towards her –

Tova threw the VHR-38 clear from her ear and silence returned.

Her chest heaved, heart pumping. The trees stood like watching sentinels, the clearing empty. There was no sign of movement anywhere nearby. But there had been, in those sounds. She stared at the sound processor, now dormant on the ground, a smoking gun.

"What was that?" Ki's voice came back, anxiously.

Tova swiped the VHR back off the grass and ran.

7

"Wait! Slow down, what did you hear? Stop!"

Tova ignored the voice, but she did slow as the path took her back into the open, wary of drawing attention.

She was losing her mind – she had to be losing her mind.

"Can you still hear me?"

Those screams could *not* be real. That meant his voice was likely not real, either.

As she marched, a sudden movement near her head made her reel to the side, one arm up for protection. Chest rising and falling in short breaths, she watched a dark shape flutter between the trees – that blurry bird again, wings moving too fast for her to make it out. It settled above her head, concealed in the shadows of tree branches.

"I can give you a piece of Very Good Advice," Ki said. "Don't use that machine. It's hurting you."

Tova raised her voice to reply, "Did you hear it too? Tell me you heard it too!"

"I heard nothing," Ki answered, gravely. "What was it?"

"Screams," Tova replied tremulously, admitting it to herself. "Everywhere...screams..."

She turned, staring accusingly at the trees before starting away again. Mei started talking, her Japanese remarks edged with questioning and concern. Tova hurriedly followed the path around a bend as Ki answered Mei. Their voices got quieter the quicker Tova moved. More distant. They weren't really there, they couldn't be. It was all part of some terrible mistake Mogami had made. The voices faded to silence as she reached a delicately arched bridge, mirrors of still water stretching either side of it.

Tova slowed to take out her phone, pleading it to have signal, but there was nothing. She'd find Ali from the Shinjuku Deaf Club. Contact the hospital. She couldn't wait hours for everyone back home, she needed someone now.

"Tova, please wait," Ki's voice came again, loud, as another bird-flutter made Tova twist fearfully around. This shape shot under the bridge, gone as quickly as it appeared. It didn't come out the other side. "Where are you going?"

Tova clutched her head. They'd poisoned her, corrupted her, done something terrible. As the emotion rose, a senseless noise escaped her lips.

"Tova! Please!" Ki called. "Keep calm!"

"Calm?" Tova shouted, thrusting a finger back the way she'd come. "What was that?"

"I don't know," Ki said, joined by an aggressive suggestion from Mei. He snapped a curse at her and said, "Tell me. What did you hear?"

Tova breathed deeper, steadied the shuddering of her chest.

"Screams," she said again. "They were coming at me. They were..." She shook on the spot, wiping at her own arms as though feeling the touch of those monstrous sounds. She shook her head. "I have to get away."

"We can help you with that," Ki insisted, and Tova froze.

That was a response, a real response. And not the first – he had answered her question before. She felt the words slip out. "You can hear me?"

Ki was quiet.

Tova backed into the bridge's low barrier and clutched it for support. She searched the park with her eyes: a place of delicate flowers and sculpted trees. A serene vista packed with hiding places, but not on this bridge. There was a pair of women, walking and chatting on the far bank. A jogger off beyond them. No one close enough to hear her. Tova said, "Where are you...you're not here..."

"First, we need to make sure you're safe. Mei will secure a new hotel for you, yes? Whatever you just experienced –"

"I didn't imagine it," Tova hissed.

"I believe you," Ki replied, perfectly serious. And Tova paused, realising she believed *him*. He hadn't assured her she was hearing things, hadn't tried to play down her fears about those men. The opposite – he'd called them no ordinary criminals. And he'd said he needed to make sure she was safe. He was no random stranger.

Tova demanded, "What's going on?"

Mei answered for Ki, but not in English. Whatever she said, it left Ki without a response for a moment. When he laughed, it sounded forced. He said, "I don't think we can draw conclusions. It's possible, though – just possible – with your hearing, and the HiWave – those men –"

"*What is going on?*" Tova repeated. The two women across the water stopped to look her way, their familiar expressions of alarm clear even at this distance. She must've shouted it, and the volume had silenced Ki.

"May I make a suggestion?" he ventured carefully. "We need privacy. Far away from those men. If I can guide you safely back to your apartment –"

"If you're real," Tova cut in, straining to keep her voice lower, "why can't I see you? I want to see you. Show me you're real."

She was met with the quiet foreign whispers of the two voices, as the far-off women continued their walk. It was like looking through a window to another world – their gentle amble through a beautiful park; how could this place harbour those screams and these bodiless voices?

"I will give you my phone number," said Ki, having concluded his discussion with Mei. "You can confirm I am real with that. Text messages would prove I exist, yes?"

"What – no – why?" Tova said. "That doesn't –"

"I'll give you the number now, please be ready," he said, talking too fast for her to protest. As he started reciting the number, she hurried to open her phone and enter it. When he was done, he said, "Call it."

"I've got no signal..."

A brief pause. "Go to a café near the apartment building. You can use their internet, yes? Check my number and contact your friends while we see about getting your things out of that building. It's not safe there now."

"I can't just –"

"Tova, please trust me," he continued. His voice came lightly, as though this was almost a game, and she was silly to take it so seriously. "We're connected by a strange bit of coincidence but also great fortune. I cannot explain your hearing, but it is affected by the HiWave, which suggests one thing. The chances are very high that those men were a special kind of police. A bad kind, but ones who we know well how to avoid. Please, go to a café, wait for me there, and we will take care of you. Everything is fine."

Tova scoffed back her disbelief. Screams and unseen voices

and now *police* – it was insane. She shook her head, issues only mounting as she gave it some thought. The suggestion the authorities were dangerous would utterly isolate her. Half the addresses in her notebook were connected to Japan's emergency services. And those men didn't look like police. Ki was playing with her – at best.

If he was real, he might be trying to get her alone. But she was pretty well alone *here*, why bother sending her back to her things, to use the internet...

If he *wasn't* real, it made more sense. The rapid descent into madness naturally included paranoia about the people that could help her. Either he was out of his mind or she was. In both cases she needed real help, not the help of some invisible voice. She said, "I'll go back to the hospital. I have to."

There was no reply. Ki's breath, even, was gone.

Tova continued, "Those men weren't police, I don't believe it. Why would they be?"

Still no answer. The world was silent again, and as Tova's eyes ran over the park she realised he was gone. It was all gone – the frantic account of this apparently friendly stranger, along with the threat of whatever those screaming noises were. She looked at the bridge under her feet, wondering if that bird was gone, too.

With the renewed silence came a chill, despite the high sun.

"Ki?" Tova ventured quietly. "Are you there?"

Without any response, she returned her gaze to the phone.

Well. There was no harm in trying this number, was there?

Seated in a brown diner, whose ugly smell combined burnt grease, cheap coffee and plastic, Tova couldn't bring herself to commit her situation to text. Ethan hadn't believed her before, would anyone believe her now? No one was online yet, so they would read her rambling messages as they woke, semi-consciously discovering what? Men chased her from her apartment, a voice started talking to her in the park, screams knocked her off her feet – none of it provable. And she'd left the hospital with confirmation she could *not* hear. Ethan would say she was imagining it, Mum would panic that the operation had had awful side effects and Dad would start making furious demands of Mogami, further pissing them off. The only person with the imagination to cope with this was Ren, and she was starting her new job. The distraction of

Tova fretting from Japan would ruin her first day, which she was already stressed about.

Using the diner's Wi-Fi, Tova wrote and rewrote and deleted a dozen messages to Ren before finally settling on one she thought broached the subject without making her look utterly mad: *The operation's gone wrong but I'm still hearing a voice. And something much worse. Also some men came looking for me. Wish you were here.*

It still sounded loopy.

The reality, she realised, was that she needed Ki back to make sense of this. She needed to go back to the apartment, to see if there was anything to be afraid of, and it was difficult to make a move without further input from him.

She'd pinged a message to his number and received a rapid answer: *Hey! I'm using a phone, I must be real, right?* Not convinced she wasn't hallucinating too, Tova showed the phone to a waitress and, after a little pantomiming and clumsy explanation about being deaf and having difficulty reading, got the waitress to transcribe the message onto a piece of notepaper. Every letter was accurate. So whatever else Tova might be dealing with, Ki existed, at least in some form that could use a phone.

Tova rubbed her eyes wearily. It wasn't enough. Ethan was right: after an operation and her long journey, who was to say what state her mind was in. She trawled the internet and found no evidence of a headset called a HiWave, nor any evidence that the VHR or stem cell therapy had anything to do with telephone signals. The closest she got were old stories about dental implants that tuned in to radios. Irrelevant. She watched people making calls in the café, including the waitress using a landline and someone on a Skype call, and heard nothing from any of them. This phenomenon was specific to Ki, which made it all the less likely. And he'd started out unable to hear her, then somehow could? Able to see her, with no way she could see him? The best explanation was that she'd been talking to that bird following her; it had gradually got closer. Get real.

The phone vibrated. Ki's number, at last. A text: *Ready?*

Tova hesitated. However his presence added up, he wasn't trapping her, was he? How would it make sense, she'd been alone all this time, why go through all this... Tova needed to go back. She typed: *Yes.*

Little animated dots showed he was writing.

A longer message appeared: *They are leaving. It doesn't look good – I really urge you to gather your things and relocate. Mei already has a hotel for you, or you can go somewhere else – we will help, whatever you decide.*

Tova fought back her reservations. She wanted to believe he was genuine. The world had delivered someone to help her, when she needed it most.

Another text appeared: *All clear. Might have hours or minutes, go now.*

Just in case, Tova took a screenshot of Ki's texts and erased her last draft to Ren. She attached the picture and wrote, instead: *Think some people were in my apartment. Don't know why. This guy's helping me check it out – if I disappear or die, avenge me.*

No time to wait for anyone to wake up now. This was it. Tova the Trooper.

Tova gawked at the state of her apartment. She made a sound, probably loud enough to be heard down the hall, and covered her stupid mouth with a hand. Any doubts she'd had about the men disappeared. Her clothes were strewn across the floor. The pockets on a pair of jeans were turned inside out. The bedsheets were asunder, all the drawers and cupboard doors open.

They'd gone through *everything*.

Creeping in, Tova kept an eye on the kitchen counter, the only place someone could be hiding. Her hands shook as she bundled her clothes into her wheeled pink suitcase. She could barely grasp the zip with her fingers trembling.

Trying not to think, she gave the room one quick going-over, checking under the bed and in the cupboards. She left the keys on the counter, no way she was coming back. This part was real – the men had come for her – they had gone through her things, looking for something. No idea what, nothing was missing, they wanted *her*, information about *her*. They might be as dangerous as Ki said, and they'd seen her flight details, her apartment invoice – they would know exactly who she was now. Might have connections elsewhere, in the police, watching people she might go to. Where could she go? A map to Ali's address was with her other travel documents, would they look there? The hospital? No, *that* was the first place they'd look.

Still no one online on her phone, dammit.

The British Embassy, that's where she'd go. Stranded in Tokyo, idiot girl with a disability, out here alone, this is what international spies were really for, right? Extract me, James Bond. But was that too obvious? These guys couldn't stake out *everywhere*. Descending in the lift, Tova wrote another message to Ren: *They've been in my place, worried about going to the police, should I go to the British Embassy?*

She held off messaging her parents. This warranted a call.

The lift doors opened at the ground floor and Tova dreaded the open space ahead. She should have scrimped together more money for a hotel with a receptionist to call for a taxi. She hurried outside with her head down and blundered into a woman carrying a dozen shopping bags.

"Hey!" Ki's voice cut into Tova's panicked attempts to apologise. She skidded and checked other people nearby, scowling faces quickly walking to important places. "Ah yes – it works; I am broadcasting without a call this time. Excellent. Flag a taxi, I'll read out the hotel's address. Best I don't send it in a message."

A teenager bumped into Tova, walking with a couple of others in tatty denims, chains hanging from their belts. He gave her an irritated look but said something to his friends and they all laughed as they continued.

"You hear me, don't you?" Ki continued. "Mei secured a hotel for you, like I promised – a proper one. Maybe the only place in this city you can safely go right now."

The only safe place? Surely the embassy was safe?

Tova's shoulder was knocked again, making her shriek. This time the man, a head shorter, was the one bowing and apologising, as Tova moved to perch half-off the curb to avoid more collisions. Amongst the cars rolling past, a couple of distinctive yellow taxis stood out. She waved at one, empty, but it kept going. She waved at another, more dramatically. Other pedestrians parted around her now; if the thugs returned, she'd stand out like a giant clown.

"If you don't want the hotel," Ki said, rapidly, "at least promise one thing. Do not use your passport, or your real name. These men will use those things to find you. Wherever you go."

Tova scanned past disdainful, preoccupied people, her eyes travelling up the grimy concrete wall of her apartment block. Near a window above, she spotted the fuzzy shape of a large beetle, in the shadow of a crack. She whispered, "Where are you...you're not here..."

"Tova, did you hear me? If those men catch you, you don't walk away."

And she was supposed to feel safe going to a hotel arranged by a voice in her head? Ethan would have a heart attack. Mum would call her a poor dear thing. The British Embassy could deal with Japanese police, couldn't they?

As a third taxi approached, Tova jumped and waved. This one swerved, lights blinking.

"It's a fine hotel," Ki assured. "You'll like it there – *top notch*."

Tova trotted to the trunk as the driver popped it open. She probed her pockets for her notebook, for the embassy address, as Ki continued: "There, we can discuss what is going on."

She frowned. That was to say he had answers, whoever, wherever he was. He claimed to know who those men were and why they wanted her. He might even know why her hearing was screwed. *Think*. Where would the embassy get her? She could hide there while she sucked up to Uncle Larry to lend her cash for an earlier flight home, or otherwise, most likely, get sent back here once it was decided the men were gone. Might they give her a room in the consulate? Some fool girl, never travelled before, running scared at the first sign of trouble.

Tova got in the car, indicating her ear to make her deafness clear to the driver. The man's smile faded. He raised his hands in a questioning shrug and said something she didn't read on his lips. She ran her fingers over the notepad. Run, or try to get ahead of this...she wished someone else was here with her. Anyone.

Ki recited a short, simple address in Japanese.

The driver waited.

Tova cleared her throat. If Ki was real, they could discuss this. If he wasn't, well, the address wouldn't make any sense. She slowly recited it and the taxi driver nodded, knowingly.

8

Nakameguro stood in calm contrast to the luminescent chaos that Tokyo had offered Tova so far. The taxi crossed a canal lined with large but delicate trees and weaved past expensive-looking shops into a maze of narrow streets. The address led to a four-storey white-washed block, adorned only by a sign in Japanese. Tova stood alongside her bag as the car pulled away, the street empty of people. The air here was as still as in the park. Behind a hint of petrol, it smelt delicately sweet and floral. Discreet, calm, welcoming. Almost enough to allay the fact that Tova had fled her official Japanese residence on the directions of a voice in her head. Ki hadn't spoken to her throughout the journey, giving her time to resume doubting his existence.

"I will explain." Ki's voice returned.

Tova instinctively signed her response, *You're here?* Recalling his earlier comments, about her "hand language" – *adorable* – she repeated it out loud, "You're here?"

"Nearby," Ki answered, able to hear her again. There were trees along the street, low walls by the other squat buildings. Many places to hide. Tova's roaming eyes rested on the luggage. Perhaps a hearing device? The bag had been in the boot during the ride...

"Are you tracking me?" Tova said.

"No." Ki sounded amused. "I am close, that's all."

"So show yourself."

"I cannot. You like this area? It is a beautiful hotel, we chose it especially."

Tova frowned, not liking that he'd moved so quickly on, but her eyes were drawn to the doorway ahead. Through the glass double doors sat a marble entrance hall. She said, "I can't afford it."

"It's a gift," Ki told her. "Or an apology, for the wrong my country has done you. No strings."

Tova shook her head. Nothing like this came for free.

"The internet is safe here, the neighbourhood too. Those men will not find you. We even have you under new, safer credentials."

"What?" Tova said. Looking at a real hotel, faced with a *gift*. This was moving way too fast. "*How?*"

"Go inside and I will explain."

"Will I come back out again?" Tova replied. This was how they got you, wasn't it? Friendly words, gifts, slowly tying you into a fiendish, horrific trap where you ended up missing in the middle of China, serving drinks naked to men in animal masks. Except *they* weren't usually voices in your head. He'd have to be a very enterprising sex trafficker to have somehow corrupted her experimental hearing operation. And he took her comment as a joke, chuckling.

"You might want to stay inside, true, it is *most opulent*."

"And you'd pay for it, just like that."

"Ah, it is nothing to me."

"No? Who are you? Why can't I see you?"

His patient breathing sounded so close. He said, "It is the way it must be."

"I don't care what you look like," Tova assured. "As long as you look like *something*. Whatever your reasons for hiding, however you're doing it, I would never judge you for how you look – I need to see you, I need to understand this – you're not invisible, there's no way –"

"I'm not telling you I'm invisible." He added, as an amused afterthought, "And *I* am not ashamed of my appearance." Like the suggestion was ridiculous. As though it was a concern for other people? Her? Tova frowned at her own haphazard clothing...waistcoat and stripy trousers, pulled on carelessly in the flurry of leaving this morning...

"Then what is it?" she said.

When he didn't answer, Tova turned on the spot. She walked to the side, leant over a short wall, paced to look around a tree. Like a game of hide and seek, with occasional looks back to her bag. She checked behind a large bin, even crouched by a parked car. As she started to cross the road, aiming at another low wall, the door to the hotel opened. A woman in uniform smiled out at Tova, checking on her unusual behaviour. Tova edged unapologetically back to her bag by the side of the road, as the receptionist approached and bowed. She said something that looked like *Good day*, then a question, a name. Miss Valentina?

Tova started to shake her head, but Ki whispered, "Yes you are. Valentina Joyce."

She kept staring at the beaming receptionist, unsure what to do with this information.

"It's a safe name to use," Ki said. "And you can use the hotel's internet, contact your family and friends, tell them where you are. Let everyone know your location, but be careful with your name. When you are satisfied, we can talk in your room."

"A safe name..." Tova echoed, imagining a scenario where those invisible screaming beasts were hunting her identity.

The receptionist's head tilted questioningly. "Excuse me, madam?"

Tova feigned ignorance, pointing at her ears and said, "I don't hear."

The woman's smile broadened and she signed, incredibly, in British Standard, *Apologies, Miss Valentina, I did not know. I am trained in many languages.*

Tova was too dumbstruck to resist the receptionist offering to take her bag; Ki whispered an explanation, "Mei chose well, yes?"

Ignoring him, she followed the receptionist into the polished corridor, all the way to a wide mahogany desk with a wafer-thin computer. The burgundy walls were trimmed with spotless brass, and the carpet felt soft enough underfoot to sleep on. Opulent was right.

The receptionist collected a keycard and placed a leather folder open on the counter, a booking form with a space for a signature. Tova scanned the text, neatly printed Japanese with English translations. Name: *Valentina Joyce*; home address somewhere in Bristol. Booked online, credit card payment already taken – the last four unfamiliar digits showing. Tova couldn't stop staring at that. If this was conjured by an imagined voice, she was desperate to know how Alter-Tova could have wrangled this.

The beaming receptionist tapped a pen against the signature line and Tova took it.

About to commit identity fraud.

She waited for Ki's voice to encourage her, to insist on this being the only way, that this luxury accommodation was purely in the interests of evading a conspiracy. He said nothing, though. She put the pen down and asked in sign language, "Wi-Fi?"

The receptionist nodded and offered an information slip with a password. Tova connected her phone to the internet and apologised as she moved away from the counter. A dozen concerned messages pinged up. Ren was awake: *What the hell is going on? Where are you? Talk to me, Tova!*

Tova replied: *I'm safe.*

A Skype call popped up: Mum. Tova went to a shelf and propped up the phone on its kickstand. She answered the video call to find her mother dancing in flustered sign language. Tova signed, "I'm okay, Mum."

"Okay? Ren says men broke into your room!"

"I wasn't there. They didn't take anything."

"Where are you now?" A look of confusion. "Did you go to the embassy?"

"Another hotel. In a different district. Far away. Safe."

Her mum paused, thoughtful for a second, then stopped signing to say something. No way Tova could read her lips with this quality video. She shook her head, getting a frown and more signing: "You're not wearing the processor?"

"It went wrong," Tova signed.

"Oh heavens. What's happened?"

"The doctors don't know. It's confusing, and weird."

"Where are you, exactly? How did you get there? Have you contacted the Deaf Club?"

"I'm fine," Tova signed with a smile, unsettled by her mother's rising concern.

"You poor thing," Mum hurriedly continued. "We knew this would happen. You can't go through this alone – you don't have to. I'll contact Uncle Larry, maybe I can still get a flight."

We knew this would happen? "Give me a minute."

"I know what you're thinking, Tova, sweet Tova. You don't have anything to prove."

It was concern, but the same concern as Ethan's, wasn't it? Poor Tova, cracking under the pressure. And there was no way they could afford to come, else her parents would've joined her in the first place, no matter how much Tova insisted she could do this without them. Hell, Uncle Larry probably couldn't even afford to lend them the money. That meant the more concerned Mum got, the more likely it was she'd contact someone, anyone, to look out for Tova, and potentially blow whatever Ki had managed to secure here. She needed answers before this ship got torpedoed. Tova's hands moved ahead of her thoughts: "I got my money back from the last apartment and they helped set me up here. As an apology. But the men searched my things so I'm using a different name. I'm handling myself, and I've got another appointment to reassess my hearing – it's all going to be okay, everything is fine..."

And just like that, she was ready to sign for this hotel.

9

Her new view was a world apart from Kabukicho's bedlam. The buildings were smaller, less metal and glass, more designer trees and creeping ivy. Calm, reflecting the mood that Tova had chosen to adopt. As a single concession to her family's concerns, she allowed her father to contact the British Embassy to let them know what she was going through, and offered no objection to him chasing Mogami Industries. Otherwise, she insisted, she would quite happily take care of herself. She even played things down to Ren, who was getting ready to go out but worried she shouldn't work at all, in case Tova needed her. Tova didn't explain the screams, nor exactly what was going on with Ki, and had finally ended up in a room twice the size of the apartment she'd left behind, with a bed big enough to sleep three, trying to convince herself that yes, this was the right choice.

Get her head straight first. Let everyone at home worry later.

Once the receptionist left her, Tova searched her bag, then the room, behind the doors, under the bed, in the drawers. There was a dark wooden desk and a freestanding bath fit for a queen, but no sign of bugs or cameras. No sign of Ki, who'd not said a word since she entered the building.

Still, her gut told her he was nearby.

Finally settling in the middle of the room, Tova called out, "Ki?"

"Yes." His voice came directly into her ear. She twisted but there was no one there. "Welcome. Is it to your liking?"

Tova studied her feelings. It wasn't ridiculous to feel fortunate now, was it? You heard stories about people who narrowly avoided holiday disaster only to have some generous Samaritan put them up, didn't you?

Granted, those stories were usually more easily explained than this: the charity of a kindly hotel manager or a quick-thinking tour guide, for example. Someone you could at least see. Ki was nothing like those possibilities, and she sensed, somehow, he really was nearby. The feeling in the hairs on your arms, a tickle on the back of the neck, when something was happening that you couldn't see. It didn't make sense and she wondered if she should be more afraid. She said, "You're going to tell me who you are, now?"

"Ah – oh," Ki replied merrily. "You can call me snowflake."

Tova waited for a punchline.

"Because I have fallen for you."

This was unreal: a luxury room courtesy of a disembodied voice making cheesy jokes, in between people hunting her. She said, "You're in this room? Right now?"

No answer.

"If I'm going crazy, how did I get booked in here?"

"You're not going crazy," Ki said. "We arranged it while we waited for the men to leave your other building. And you do not need to be afraid, I will leave you alone soon enough, once I have shared something with you. One more thing Mei is preparing."

"Is it an explanation?" Tova answered quickly, hopefully. "About those screams, those men you call police, my hearing *you*?" When Ki didn't respond at once, Tova's hand rose again to the scar on her head. The longer he didn't explain, the more she dreaded the truth. Those screams had come at her with the balled fury of something that hated the fact she knew it was there. Those men, too, running into her building. "What did they do to me?"

"The doctors? Nothing intentionally, I don't think," Ki said. "If Mogami had any idea this was possible, they would have been watched, I am sure. But those police were already in that building, you said. Possibly, you were in the wrong place when the results of your surgery triggered one of their alerts."

"Alerts? For what? How do you know about this stuff?"

Another pause, and Tova realised these hesitations were him deciding how much to share. He hadn't been watching her by chance. He said, "I have more than a passing interest in Dr Eguchi's work, it is true. Not because I thought it could produce these results. This reaction, between his experiment and my people's technology..."

"Your people?" Tova frowned. No answer. "You're not from here? The police –"

"Are afraid of such things," Ki cut in. "They control knowledge of what they consider unnatural."

"Are *you* unnatural?" Tova said, not quite sure as she said it where the question came from.

Ki made an awkward sound, and Tova realised there was something in the thought she'd blurted out. He said, "I meant the leap between your hearing implant and my headset. Whatever caused its malfunction; Mogami's research has attuned a human ear to a HiWave? The Obake Police would wish to contain such an unusual event."

Tova dwelt warily on his choice of words. Unnatural, the human ear, contain...

"It is possible," Ki continued carefully, "that they stumbled across your situation while routinely scanning communications in the building. Or they may have already suspected you would have an unusual reaction, for whatever reason. Did you say something that might have alerted such people?"

Tova had first feared it was hearing Ki that had brought the men to her, but no: the men came running after she'd chatted with Ethan. When she was trying to explain what she was going through. But who would take that seriously? Ethan hadn't. Reliving those moments, the men charging into the building, Tova sat down on the bed. "Why would they suspect me? There's been dozens of candidates – Mogami have testimonials on their website – why should I be special?"

"We would have to understand how this reaction –"

"No, *you* said I was special, *you* were watching me – why?"

"Ah." Ki gave a light laugh. "I know you are special not because of this. You are so brave, and bold, and beautiful, true, but it is because you are from Ordshaw that I took this interest. Serendipity, as you say. Dr Eguchi's miracle work, with you, and their most special reward, involving another very special visitor from Ordshaw."

Tova suddenly sensed what he was about to say, and it was going to make things worse.

"You must be so excited, to meet the most wonderful, the majestic, Natalie Reid?"

Looking sideways at the window, Tova half-expected to see the pop star's face somewhere out there, ever-present, as it had been in Kabukicho. *Of course* this had to involve her, because that was the best way to make things completely surreal. Out in Japan with all hell stirring, bring in an Ordshaw council kid turned gazillionaire superstar. Natalie Reid's songs spoke of poverty and ugliness, while her brand promoted gritty urban fashion, the English counterpart to the futuristic wonder of modern Tokyo. Tova had barely given the star a thought since first visiting the hospital, the dream of meeting a star a very distant concern. She wasn't sure Mogami were even going to honour that part of their deal now, but somehow it had captured Ki's imagination.

Was that all? Ki was a superfan, looking for a chance to meet Natalie Reid? It's the sort of scheme Ren might concoct; befriend a nobody with a disability and ride to fame on the coattails of her recovery story. Ren had once drafted a letter proposing Natalie write an album aimed entirely at her deaf fans, imagining it would bring Ripton's Second Thursday Deaf Club untold riches. In reality, all Ren had wanted was a response. The draw might be even stronger for some Japanese recluse.

"She is a marvel, yes?" Ki said, eagerly. "A prodigy from Ordshaw, the same as you. What a union your meeting will be!"

"Mogami aren't likely to arrange it, now, not if my hearing's not working."

"Nonsense!" Ki cried. "Things have become complicated, but it is still possible. She would want to please a fan *especially* in harder times, no? And if Mogami hesitate, we can spur them on. Mei can do wonderful things with a computer, wonderful things."

So there it was, the thing this voice in her head wanted. Tova tried to decide how upset to be. These were extreme measures for Ki to take to help him get close to Natalie Reid, but in principle at least it was little different to Dad inviting her for a shopping trip in central Ordshaw so he could park in the Disabled spots. And it was leagues above sex trafficking. Tova found herself picking at her stitches again. It was more complicated, though, considering the other things Ki had said now. "Why do you want to meet her?" she asked.

"Ah, no!" Ki quickly cut in. "I cannot meet her myself! I did not mean for *us* to have this contact. I couldn't possibly get close to Ms Reid. I only thought you might wish to bring her something, a token of kindness, and I had something that might help you. Local crafts."

Tova took a moment. "A local craft being something to do with your people who want to remain hidden?"

Quiet again.

"If I explain –"

"You promised you would."

Another pause. "Yes. But the Obake would find you. If not them, then my people would. I'm so sorry. I have done this wrong, I have told you things – I should not have spoken at all. I was surprised by the HiWave, by all this."

His people, he'd said it again. Unnatural. Knowledge of the men chasing her. She said, "But you knew who these police are, what exactly they were searching for in the first place? Why my..." Tova thought of the screams. Barely wanting to acknowledge them. He claimed to know these things and she could hear him – was it connected to what else she'd heard?

"Ah!" Ki made a happy announcement. "Now. It is here. Let me show you something. I think this will help, and with it I hope you will better trust me. I cannot explain your hearing or these men, but this –"

"What?" Tova prompted.

"Okay..." Ki cleared his throat. "Open the door. Please. It waits in the hall."

Tova looked up suddenly. Someone had been out there? She hadn't noticed shadows under the door. She hesitantly stood. What was there now? Something to do with her hearing, an offering connected to his alleged advanced technology? Praying to whatever controlled the universe that it might clarify *something*, Tova went to the door and hesitated with her hand on the handle.

Ki became excited: "Freshly delivered. You are the first to see this, okay? A prototype."

Tova's curiosity was piqued. Prototype was good. She opened the door and leant cautiously out. The hallway was empty, no one there in either direction. There was indeed something on the floor, though. Her heart fell. "Socks? A pair of socks?"

"Yes."

No explanation followed.

"Pick them up."

Tova crouched and reached a finger towards the pair of navy-blue socks, crisply laid out as though ironed. She prodded them. No surprises there, so she lifted them. Lightweight while also thick. With the way the material moved and caught the light, they looked utterly seamless. Incredibly soft and smooth. There was a single strip of paler blue which would accentuate the natural line of the foot, but there was no sign of stitching, no break in the material whatsoever. It wasn't the smoothly reflective surface of silk or a cotton matte. It was something else.

"Try them on."

"It's a pair of socks."

"Try them *on*."

Tova checked up and down the hall again, definitely no one around. She backed off into the room, closing the door, and stared at the socks. She considered that this might be the appropriate time to simply stop everything and scream. She could, perhaps, keep screaming until this all went away, or the world cracked and split apart. She had moved a mile a minute into a scenario that had her completely flummoxed and the voice in her head had graduated from talks of conspiracy to fawning over a pop star to trying on socks and she Could Not Cope.

"Try them," Ki insisted, speaking softer now, "and it'll start to make sense."

Tova shook her head, not to refuse him but to refuse the situation. A dream, an impossible, surreal dream, that's all it was. Through the looking glass. She sat back on the bed and took off her Converse and the socks she'd been wearing. Holding this new pair, she reconsidered how impressive they were and felt inadequate. She'd been running around Tokyo in various forms of panic – she should wash.

"Try them!" Ki exclaimed, barely able to contain himself.

Tova fumbled them on quickly, to stop his noise, and cooed.

A rung above *weird*. The socks simultaneously held her closely and barely felt present. Most strange of all, they looked incredible. Tova couldn't recall ever being impressed by a sock. This pair had her eyes bulging.

Forgetting herself, she signed her questions, *How did you...what is...*

"Yes!" Ki said triumphantly. "That is it! You understand – surely you understand!"

With everything she was going through, *socks* were supposed to make her understand? Tova said, "Is this what you want me to give to Natalie Reid?"

"Heavens no," Ki whispered.

"What, then?" Tova wriggled her toes. Why did the socks felt *so good*?

"Fantastic, aren't they? So special."

"Yeah..."

"You look incredible in them, yes? A goddess. *This* is the future, and it is also the why. We can do great things." He kept going, caught up in patter. "Across all the islands, there is nothing so exquisite. Mount Rishiri is not wicked, it is to be respected and revered. This work, above all else. Yet *this* is what they fear, our excellence. They seek to hide a thousand secrets, ours the least worthy."

Tova refocused, tried to register and interpret every word, realising he was forgetting himself in his passion. She said, "They're *amazing*. Why would anyone fear this?"

"Because humans *never* understand!" Ki exclaimed.

Tova's jaw dropped. What the actual fuck?

She sat totally still, Ki's worried breathing proof he'd slipped up. He muttered hurriedly, "Please, accept this gift as our conclusion. We are both tired – I must leave. Rest, and know you are safe. Consider the concert, I beg you –"

"No!" Tova stood, raising her voice. "This doesn't explain –"

"I will be far away, and you will be safe, only if you avoid using your name."

"Wait!" Tova shouted. "This isn't an answer!"

He didn't respond.

"Ki! Talk to me! What's going on?"

Tova remained standing. Refusing, for the moment, to accept that the silence was back.

Ki strode into his new workspace. This hideout was larger than the crawl space they'd secured in the Kabukicho block, and far enough from Tova that she couldn't accidentally listen in on his calls again, but it had been a pain to relocate to. It'd take half a day to get the weaver properly calibrated again. Another half day getting the lighting and temperature right. To say nothing of all the damn wiring, all those computer monitors stacked in a wall, currently bathing Mei in light. She lolled back in his leather swivel chair.

"Why are you still here?" Ki said. "Isn't everything set up? I have work to do."

"I saw your counselling," Mei said, dryly.

"Ah" – Ki waved a hand – "it's nothing. You saw, too, that she needed some persuading?"

"That was persuasion? This engagement was never part of the plan. All this talking."

Ki started pacing. "In Ordshaw, they talk –"

"In Ordshaw, in Ordshaw." Mei stood with enough force to send the chair spinning. "One person" – she held up a finger – "talked. One. That doesn't give you free rein."

Ki smiled with acid. "Free from what? Am I waiting on permission to be brilliant?"

Mei turned her nose up, but her indignation was not quite up to his. She checked the monitors rather than hold his eyes. Tova was writing on her phone. Mei said, "The path *we* planned did not involve giving the deaf girl clothes, or telling her anything. We've got cameras, microphones, you didn't even need to get close."

"Except she can't hear this at a distance." Ki tapped the HiWave. "I adapted, as necessary. We're not brain-dead drones –"

"Don't. Don't insult me by pretending you meant to let her in on so much. You were just enjoying the opportunity, so caught up in the thought of talking with one of them."

"I told her nothing she can use! No specifics. The socks cannot be traced."

"She knows our names."

"Oh? And she'll pick a Mei out of the phone book to find you, will she? No one can –"

"That's how they found her. How they found us."

Ki paused. "What? You heard her, they were already checking the building. It wasn't anything to do with –"

"It was," Mei said, with righteous anger. "She wrote *your name* in her messages. Ki-Zero. A variation of it, anyway. They connected her to you."

Ki glowered. "I never gave her my full name, did I? Was I supposed to predict she'd hear us? Through this?" He shook the bulky headphones hanging around his neck.

"No, but you can at least try and exercise caution. *Socks*, Ki? You're getting –"

"Getting things done," Ki flared. "You want to take charge, form your own team." They were almost chest to chest, Ki a head taller but Mei stout, rugged. "Or should we go back to hiding in trees? No one recognising my work? No? You need my dreams, Mei, because you have none of your own. Do *not* question my methods."

Mei's eyes were burning but she held her tongue. Ki folded his arms, and after a moment Mei broke off to stomp to the exit, as he knew she would. She paused, seeming to force her remaining anger out, something else she wanted to discuss. He knew this was coming, wished she wouldn't. There was no way she was this upset over him talking to the girl. There was always going to be some kind of interaction with her, after all.

"In the park," Mei said. "This business with her processor, the HiWave..."

"Crossed wires," Ki said, waving a hand. "Nothing more."

Mei shook her head, but he looked away. If she had superstitious fears to voice, she could keep them; he had enough on his mind without adding Tova's messed-up hearing to the pile. No, their only problem was steering her in the right direction. Keeping her alive long enough to meet Natalie Reid. Everything else was irrelevant.

10

After an uneasy sleep, plagued by confusion and thoughts of the sounds she might hear, Tova's face lit up at the sight of Ren's name online. She bounced over the bed to prop up the tablet and Ren answered the instant she pressed call. It was dark in England, Ren in her night-shirt, lit only by her own tablet.

"It rises!" Ren announced in sign language.

"Finally!" Tova signed back. "I waited up late for you – when did you get in?"

"Half an hour ago. But your mum's been messaging me. Where are you, seriously? A palace? Looks like everyone's wrong to worry shitless about you."

Tova spun the tablet around to show off the room, then replied, "One good thing that's come out of all this. I couldn't explain it to Mum, not properly – and Ethan –"

"As if."

"Yeah. Ren, it's all weird and complicated. Look at this." Tova scooted over the bed and grabbed her new socks. She wrestled them on and held a foot up to the camera, struggling to keep her balance on the bed. Ren's face went from puzzled, through amused, back to quizzical.

"You got pulled into a fetish racket?" she signed.

"Seriously." Tova modelled a sock again. "What do you think?"

Ren stared hard. Then she sat back with a slanted smile. Resisting making another joke, but slow to come up with anything else. Her eyes were dark with tiredness.

"You're exhausted," Tova signed.

Ren shook her head. "No. Tell me about your new socks."

Tova hesitated. She'd run this conversation through her mind a dozen times, having failed to find the right way to explain her situation to anyone else. Ki's bodiless voice had given her overt hints towards an oppressed group, *his* people with *their* technology, but the internet said that Japan's history of ethnic issues and hazy civil rights laws was in the past. Nothing suggested there was any ethnic group being actively suppressed now. The Ainu people of Hokkaido – around the right area for Mount Rishiri, which Ki had mentioned – now had their own political party. No one was hunting or silencing them. That made Tova wonder whether Ki's people might not be an ethnic group at all. Considering the hotel and Ki's mysterious HiWave technology – and these inexplicably impressive *socks* – they might be underground hackers or engineers or something. Communicating with her via listening devices, microphones so advanced they were too small for Tova to find? That was one starting point: *I think I've fallen in with some reclusive hackers.* Except her earlier instinct kept looming large: maybe this guy was a recluse because he had something physical to hide. The way he'd said *human* suggested he really took his inferiority complex to an extreme. But then that gelled uncomfortably with the word *obake*, for a feeling that sat somewhere between the twin pillars of Something Supernatural and Tova's Going Crazy.

"You know I've been hearing a voice?" Tova started slowly.

Ren nodded. "And your dad finally got a response from Mogami saying they were sorry – things aren't working out. Bullshit, right? If you can hear one thing you can hear more, surely?"

"I don't know," Tova signed. "This voice comes with baggage. I haven't got into it properly with anyone yet. He sent me to this hotel. And left these socks."

"It was the mystery voice?" Ren leant closer in surprise. "Your parents think –"

"I know," Tova hurried to explain. "Because the reality is too strange. I can't see him and he's made really odd comments. He says the people who came to my apartment..." Tova stopped. Ki called them the *Obake* Police. Which, if she'd got the word right, meant *ghost*. There were heaps of creepy images and stories online relating to Japanese folklore, which brought to mind a terrifying literal connection to those screams. Distractedly, Tova signed, "You know they have a myth out here, about ghost pig babies that cast no shadow and steal your soul if they run between your legs?"

Ren's expression scarcely changed, waiting for a cue.

It was one of many curiosities. There was an invisible demon that they said followed you, matching your footprints and feeding on your fear. But Ki wasn't exactly scary. Then there was also the thing that ripped people to shreds after offering them a choice of toilet paper colours – Japan's monsters were out there. That's where Tova's mind had been going when she was struggling to settle into her new hotel. Unnatural monsters. Connecting them to a police force, or Ki, in the light of day, under her friend's watchful eye, was nuts. Tova smiled and signed, jokingly, "I heard these screams in the park, and this guy's voice got me thinking, as he won't show himself, what if I've stumbled into a world of invisible demons and witch-hunters, because whatever Eguchi put in me was hatched out of a devil's egg."

"Okay," Ren signed back, almost deadpan, "so what superpower does it give you?"

Tova shrugged. "The ability to be deathly afraid?"

Ren wasn't laughing. Just sitting there with concern. Desperate to help, barely able to keep her eyes open. She must've been on her feet all day on the movie set. Tova scolded herself; how was dragging Ren through this madness going to help? It was a failed surgery, some local hoodlums and a recluse with wild ideas who wanted to touch a pop star. The rest was her imagination. Tova smiled again, realising there was one aspect she could happily burden Ren with. She signed, "This guy, he *really* wants me to go to see Natalie Reid. Maybe to give her some socks, too? I don't know, I can't even think about that concert now."

"Wait, you're still going, aren't you?" Ren straightened up, though even this concern failed to completely wake her. "*I*" – she emphasised it, pointing firmly at herself – "will run through your legs and steal your soul if you flake."

"Mogami haven't given me a ticket yet. And why should they? It's not like I can hear, what am I going to do there? Offer Natalie the gift of an unseen man who gave me socks?"

"Get a clue! Mogami *owe* you. You can breathe the same air as her, for starters, who gives a shit about hearing?"

"Hey, Ms Reid, how do you do?" Tova signed, warmed by Ren's mood. "Want to perform for someone that can't hear you?"

"Eat a dick!" Ren signed. "If she paid to remodel a tower block in the Haverscott Estate, she'll take care of you, too!"

Tova simply smiled as Ren sat back, yawning widely. She tried to cover it with a forearm. Tova signed, "I haven't asked you about the job."

"It's good. Very good. But I'd rather be there."

"Next time."

"Next time," Ren mirrored with slow, tired nods.

"We'll talk later. Your tomorrow."

More nods, followed by signing, "But seriously. Take care. You're going back to the hospital, right?"

Tova nodded, though it had hardly been high on her list.

Ren signed, as an afterthought, "Don't die."

Tova signed off, lightened from the call, the weight of her paranoia somewhat lifted. Yes, the hospital was still her best bet. Dr Eguchi could explain why she was hearing things, and offer a concrete clue as to what was going on with Ki, seeing as her invisible friend was refusing to talk. She didn't feel in danger, at least. Ki had left her alone. She'd come and gone from the hotel a few times to explore the nearby shops. She could deal with this, explore Ki's proposals while she tried to get a handle on what was going on. He gave her this hotel and these socks. He could make a visit to the hospital happen, too.

Brushing her hair in preparation to go out, having received no answer from Ki, Tova saw the room phone light blinking, someone calling. The light had a legend: *Reception*. Unsure whether that was an alert to summon her or they had forgotten she was deaf, Tova swung her bag over her shoulder and made her way to the lobby. The bright-eyed receptionist handed over a crisp envelope, signing an explanation, "This arrived for you this morning."

Tova offered a smile of thanks and turned away to check the contents. Inside was a passport. She opened it and found her own face looking back at her, the same photo as her original – the same slightly confused look, as if she hadn't realised the picture was being taken. Hair askew, nose bigger than in reality. She turned it over a few times, marvelling at the quality; almost identical to her original in every way, bar the name (Valentina Joyce) and the other identifying details. Valentina Joyce had the misfortune of being born in Luton, which would presumably raise fewer eyebrows than Ordshaw.

It came with a simple printed note: *Just in case*.

This was a step above the subterfuge of giving a false name. The passport's existence raised two difficult truths that scuppered the calm Tova had regained from Ren: (a) Ki and Mei were definitely criminals and (b) they were fully serious about the Obake Police's reach.

As Tova considered the correct amount of despair to assign, her phone vibrated in her pocket. An answer from Ki: *The hospital is clear. Go now. Be careful what you tell them, and please do not mention me. You will be on your own – try not to use your real name!*

Tova decided there was no correct level of despair here; the only workable response was numb denial. It was frightening and unsafe, but perhaps the hospital would offer answers to the dauntingly resourceful voice in her head.

The hospital took on a new light as Tova wandered through its spotless halls. Every corner hid potential assailants, every door a possible gateway to trouble. She watched men in lab coats chatting to one another over clipboards, one of them eyeing her as she passed, and wondered if he was considering alerting someone. *This girl's not supposed to be here, don't you know she owns a fake passport?*

Tova paid more attention to the room names than she had on her earlier visits. Signs to wards, and variously stamped logos – not just Mogami but other expensive-looking brands. This was as much a research centre as a place of healing. One label read *Fusion Ward*. Something must've been lost in translation there, like the reception sign that advised *Depress the Button*. But what in a hospital did you mistake for fusion? She would ask Nurse Hamada about that one.

The look on the nurse's face when Tova arrived dismissed all such questions, though. Hamada hurried around the nurse's station with concern, no paper mask to hide it, signing, "Tova! You are not scheduled to be here."

"No?" She *was*. "The next tests – you told me –"

"But the appointment was cancelled," Hamada signed. Had her new friends erased records of her appointment, to make it safe? "And Dr Eguchi..." Hamada looked over her shoulder. Tova caught the worry in her eyes. Hamada collected herself and carefully signed, "Dr Eguchi is not here. He is not in today. You will have to come back."

"I'm only here for a week. How can he take time off?" Tova

feigned indignation in her expression and taut hand movements, but her thoughts ran elsewhere. Something wasn't right.

"It was unplanned," Hamada signed. "I am not sure where he is."

The nurse stalled, and Tova waited for more.

"We were contacted by your embassy. Did you tell them something? You had concerns?"

Tova shook her head. She expected her dad had given the embassy a story, but it seemed strange they'd follow up here, and not with her. She signed, "What did they want?"

"To talk to you. They explained nothing else."

Was that why Eguchi wasn't around? Worried that someone was going to start asking questions? Tova signed, "I changed hotel, they were probably checking everything is okay."

Hamada studied Tova's face for a lie. Tova raised her eyebrows with innocent encouragement and the nurse's face softened. She signed, "I see. Your case is unusual, and it was worrying that they took an interest."

Tova left it there, the nurse's caginess and Eguchi's absence flashing EXIT signs in her mind. But if there were alarms blaring, she needed some idea why. She signed, "There are more tests we can do, aren't there? Without the doctor?"

Hamada considered it, then nodded. "You have the processor with you?"

Tova put a hand in her pocket, closing it over the VHR-38. With her fear of being chased and whatever Mogami might be hiding, behind all the confusion with whatever Ki wasn't telling her, she'd pushed the possibility of actually getting her ear working to the back of her mind. She hadn't switched this thing on since the park.

Her phone off, alone with Hamada in a tiny consultation room, Tova forced herself to go through the reattachment of the VHR-38. The nurse mistook her tension for hopefulness, with a pitying smile. More than once she'd tried to dampen expectations, signing that it was unlikely they could turn this around. As Tova clipped the processor in, she breathed harder, deeper, ready to throw it away the second those screams tore through her. She flipped the switch.

Nothing.

No crackling, no screams. Hamada's mouth moved in silence.

Tova exhaled relief, as the nurse's face fell. She knew then that these tests would be useless. Ki was right: they had no idea what they'd done.

Half an hour of experiments followed, including tools that monitored for physical responses and all manner of audio stimuli, such as radios, televisions, phones and other apparatus. As they continued, Tova tentatively signed questions about the possibility of picking up the sounds of a phone call or a wireless network, and Hamada returned confused responses, insisting that even if these ideas weren't impossible, these tests would expose such things. Tova asked if there were any sound waves – or anything else – that the implant might interact with, outside their understanding.

Again a wary look from Hamada. She signed, "I am so sorry. We have tried everything."

Would knowing about the HiWave and its rogue technologist owner help? They'd already done what they could – Ki had suggested himself they would not understand. Tova signed tentatively, "I did hear things. Lots of things."

"I know," Hamada signed. "The surgery was successful. Briefly. And you may continue to hear at occasional moments, perhaps clearly, but it will not last."

Hamada signed that it appeared, despite initial appearances, that Tova's body had rejected the injected hormones. She insisted they had regrown hairs inside Tova's ear, impossibly, and those hairs were responsive, at least physically. But whatever responses they produced, her brain could not process them as sound. So what, Tova was left thinking, had they done? What had they grown in her, whose messages her brain couldn't interpret? Surely those hairs did *something*?

Tova finally signed, "Did you give me the wrong hairs? Nose hair in my ear canal?"

The nurse averted her eyes, as though not seeing the question, so Tova gesticulated more broadly to get her attention. "What did you put in me? It wasn't natural."

Hamada signed, "It was developed in the strictest conditions. The components were controlled –"

"What are the components?" Tova cut in. "Do you know?"

The nurse's face turned guiltily away. Trapped in a corner, realisation in her eyes that Tova was touching on the reality of whatever they had done.

"You don't know yourselves, what it did to me," Tova signed slowly.

Hamada bowed her head, conceding the truth.

"What's going to happen to me?"

"We've done everything we can," Hamada signed. "The surgery grant..."

"Provides no aftercare," Tova summarised. The risks were her own, the consequences too. "No follow-up, no understanding, except that it failed." Shit, Ki was right about all of it: it wasn't them, it was her. She was an abnormality that didn't fit their model, making Mogami want to cut her loose and the Obake Police want to contain her.

"When you return to Ordshaw," Hamada signed, "our experts there will see you. If you experience further effects –"

"No!" Tova signed quickly. Without a better understanding, with life getting more difficult, she might not even make it back to Ordshaw. "There has to be more you can do – here – now. Where did this research come from? Which ingredients were most dangerous? Strangest?"

Hamada frowned more severely. She signed, "What has given you such suspicions?"

Tova bowled on, "Are there people in Mount Rishiri you took something from?"

"What are you –" Hamada tried to intervene, but her eyes widened with surprise, looking over Tova's shoulder. Tova twisted in her seat, ready to dismiss whatever orderly was trying to cut in. She stopped. The trim slate suit, the grey designer stubble of his square jaw, and the cool calculation in his bespectacled eyes all worked to give the Westerner in the doorway an authoritative presence. Something told Tova he was not a member of staff.

His words formed clearly on his lips. "Can I have a word with Tova, now?"

11

Tova was rigid as the man took Hamada's seat. The room suddenly felt very small, now the nurse had left them alone. He had a woody smell, a hint of frankincense, pleasant and deeply manly.

"Sean Tasker," he said, giving her a firm handshake. Her heart fluttered at his touch: Tasker belonged on a shaving advert. His fine suit and expensive square glasses scarcely hid the square shoulders and upright posture of a man who knew how to use his body. And *Tasker*, that name paired nicely with *Tova*, didn't it? He made Ethan look like a thin, immature boy.

Tasker handed Tova a business card. Yes, she'd read the name on his lips correctly: *Sean Tasker. Agent International, Ministry of Environmental Energy.* A phone number and a crest of lions and laurels with the distinctly regal appearance of a British institution. Her job in the council took her into contact with all the arms of government, usually when they impeded local activities, but this one was a mystery. It gave Tova's heart an altogether different flutter. A man in black (well, grey, but still). Did the Obake Police have British stooges? Or did the UK have their own equivalent?

Tova forced a thin smile. Tasker smiled back, with no real feeling. His pale grey eyes were both striking and cold. Tova imagined describing him to Ren later, laughing about it.

Hey, Mr Tasker, how do you do? Quite well indeed, let me tell you. I'm an international man of mystery, here to save your life. If you can warm my heart, I might make you my wife.

No. She didn't feel like laughing now.

He started talking, seeming to admit that he knew Tova couldn't hear him, but continuing anyway. *Translator*, he said. They were waiting on a translator?

"The nurse can sign," Tova said, getting no visible response from Tasker.

He was studying her, and Tova had to look away under his gaze. He reached into his jacket and took out a small leather notebook. In his other hand, an expensive pen. He wrote something, then turned the pad around to show her: *You've heard some strange things?*

His writing was as square as his jaw.

What should she tell him? The truth? How was she supposed to know if he was here to help or abduct her? She said, "I've never heard of this Ministry."

He gave her another flash of a smile, there and gone again in an instant. He wrote, talking as he did. She caught what might be *environmental*, but his head was bowed, hard to read the rest. He showed her what he'd written: *We're responsible for environmental matters as opposed to typical human concerns.* Yes, environmental, a hundred points for Tova. Outside *human* concerns, though – minus a thousand for fear factor. He gave a slight elaboration, which she read on his lips: "Beyond politics, law, infrastructure, you understand?"

The armrest felt hard in Tova's hand; it took a moment to realise she was digging her fingers in. She imagined her understanding was not what he intended. He wanted to suggest matters outside the *built* environment, outside society. But he'd specified *human*, the same way Ki had said *human*, and Tova started picturing Japanese demons again. There was one that stalked and ate people; it had hair in its mouth.

She said, "You know about my operation?"

Tasker nodded.

"Do you know what happened to me?"

Tasker shook his head. "Tell me."

"They say they don't understand what went wrong."

"What did you hear?"

Tova scanned the card in her hands again. "Why are you interested?"

With a knowing nod, the agent wrote his explanation. He held it up for her: *It's possible Mogami's experiments crossed a few boundaries. If it affects the safety of British subjects, we have to investigate.*

That was something. He was talking about the company, the hospital, not her. Coming at this from a different angle to the men breaking into her apartment. But that didn't mean he wasn't shady. His goal might be the same: silence her for hearing strange things. Tova's jaw clenched, and Tasker picked up on it with a raised eyebrow.

"I want to help you," he said. A phrase Tova could read in her sleep. Tasker raised a finger for her patience and started writing again: *You heard something that didn't appear to be there, correct?*

Tova didn't move. Now she saw it in writing, in the hand of this *spook*, it seemed dangerously real. A road to a padded cell or to the actual source of those screams? Neither was good. He took the pad back and continued writing.

Your father filled us in on a few details. The hospital aren't taking it seriously, but you heard screams?

Tova nodded, slowly.

"I want you to stay with me," Tasker said, laying the notepad on his lap. He pointed at her, then at himself. "Tell me everything." He started listing questions, apparently to put them out there rather than get answers. Something to do with *what exactly* she heard, anything from Mogami, any *concerns* about their *research*.

These weren't probes for illicit information, were they? Maybe he really was here to protect her. She could explain her operation – the screams – without touching on Ki. She could do it without sounding like she believed it herself. Tread a line between presenting herself as a problem and discovering if this man could do something to help.

"The more you can tell me," Tasker's lips said, "the more I can do."

Could he figure it out for her? She'd come this far alone, wasn't it time to take a *real* helping hand? One that wasn't a bodiless voice.

Her posture must have softened, because his expression relaxed. Tova slipped her arm off the armrest, onto her lap, and offered a conciliatory smile. Okay, let's go. She said, "You came because I said I heard screams?"

Tasker nodded. "Yes." He said something else, too fast for her to catch, maybe *investigating*. Tova frowned: was he suggesting this was part of another investigation?

"You don't think I imagined it?" she asked, carefully.

Tasker's crystal eyes didn't leave hers. Like time had stopped. He lifted the notepad again, and said what he was writing: *I couldn't judge until I have all the details.*

Now it was Tova's turn to stare. She needed to be cautious.

Tell her family she was speaking to a government agent; check with Ki as to what was safe to say. Ki had let her take precautions; if Tasker could be trusted he would be lenient with her, too.

"Can you give me a minute?" Tova asked. He gave her a questioning look. "I've got to use the bathroom. While we wait for the translator?"

Tasker's face remained blank, before something clicked and he remembered to smile. "Of course."

He stood, smoothing his jacket as he did, his aftershave hitting her like an invitation. He held the door open and Tova walked out, under the watchful gaze of Hamada from the nurse's station. Tasker said something to her, lingering by the consultation room door as Tova dragged her feet down the hall. Hamada went back to typing at the computer as she passed, and Tova picked up her pace to the toilets. She went into a stall and locked it, sat on the toilet.

While she waited for her phone to boot up, Tova took a long pee, letting out a relieved sound, not realising how much she'd needed it. Being near Tasker had been more stressful than she'd appreciated. A shadow moved past her stall, making her go quiet. Someone else had been in there, now fleeing the discomfort of a noisy toilet-mate.

Ah, blundering crassness, my old friend.

Tova felt like laughing now. Whatever alarm bells he rang, Tasker had let her wander off; he wasn't here to corner her. He was investigating Mogami, which was a good thing. There was every possibility things would be okay.

The phone blinked to life with a message from Ki lighting up the screen.

Where the hell are you? You have to MOVE.

12

After checking the other toilet stalls, Tova pressed herself against the bathroom doors to read her other messages. Starting fifteen minutes ago, Ki had left a tirade: *Something's wrong, they're heading your way.*

Shit, he hadn't told her there was risk here.

Another message, twelve minutes ago: *Definitely heading to the hospital. Get out.*

Tova's heart was pounding. How long had she been with Tasker? More than ten minutes? Were the Obake Police alerted around the time of his arrival?

Ki's messages got more panicked from there: *Move you idiot, move!, Tova why aren't you moving?!, They're almost there!*

Tova sent a quick reply: *Phone was off. There's a man from the embassy here.*

Ki replied quickly: *Claiming to be who? SIS?*

Tova wrote: *Ministry of Environment Energy.*

Ki's response was almost instant: *Get away from him. Right now.*

Tova screwed her eyes closed. Tasker wasn't safe? She pushed the door out to scan the hall. The nurse's station was barely visible down the corridor, only Hamada's arm in view. The consulting room and Tasker were out of sight. She could go the other way, unseen. Trust Ki over her own government? Hell, how did she know for sure he was even from her government. The phone buzzed in her hand.

KI: *Obake coming in the East Wing. Exit somewhere else.*

Tova shot another look back to the nurse's station. There'd be time to rethink this later – from a distance – and she had Tasker's card. Clutching her bag to her chest, Tova briskly walked off, away from Hamada and the agent.

She checked the signs hanging from the ceiling, mostly indecipherable Japanese. The moment she spotted an arrow with English text, NORTH WARD, she accelerated and crashed into a

nurse coming the opposite way. As the nurse gesticulated angry
surprise, Tova sped up, but when she hit a pair of double doors
she skidded on the polished floor.

Tova stopped in a wide hallway with a curved counter, where
three employees in scrubs stopped a conversation with surprise.
One of them said something, and from the look of the doors
ahead, and the waiting room chairs, she understood she couldn't
continue without a reason. She scanned quickly for an Exit sign,
and spotted an icon for stairs. Waving at the nurses like an
ignorant tourist, she hurried that way.

Tova took the steps three, four at a time, faster than she'd ever
moved in Physical Education. Her heart was pounding when she
finally left a doorway and hit a wall of humid air. Outside. A van
trundled ahead of her. She scanned right and left. No idea which
side of the hospital she'd come out on, or where to go from here.

She checked her phone again. No signal now, though Ki had
got one last message in: *I'm on my way*.

Tova looked skyward, willing him to glide in on wings. That
would be something.

There was a subway sign ahead, at the base of what seemed to
be a massive shopping centre. Tova darted towards it, across the
road, between vehicles. As she reached the doors, the big man in
the bodywarmer stepped out. His eyes shared her surprise, then
her realisation. Bloody hell, what were the chances?

Tova darted away from him, into a bottleneck of people.

She pushed and shoved, her one advantage being she was about
half the width of the thug behind her. She didn't need to look back
to know he was close. She broke free and rounded a corner, then
kept running. A bus pulled in ahead – she could leap on. Trapping
herself in a box with him? Tova feigned going for the opening
door and dived aside. An arm careened into view and she ducked
to avoid it – someone knocked down by her pursuer.

A street market came up on the right. Tova pushed into an even
tighter crowd, past stalls and over tat strewn across the pavement.
She jumped a crate of fruit and almost stumbled, but kept going.
Mouths opened wide with shouts, arms waved at her. Up ahead, a
burly man in an apron stepped into her path. Dammit, was her
pursuer shouting for assistance? *Stop her stop her*.

Tova sprang down a narrow gap between stalls and found
herself in the back stores of the market – a wide open warehouse

floor, damp and dark, stinking of fish. Her shoes splashed through puddles as she aimed for a passageway ahead, a small exit doorway leading to a dark, uninviting alley. Her only chance. The metal bulkhead of a walk-in freezer pivoted open to her right, its surface vaguely reflecting her frantic advance – and the bulky, terrifying shape behind her.

Something crackled in Tova's ear and she faltered, putting a hand to her temple.

Another crackle and Ki's voice broke in.

"– that's it, keep going – I've got you –"

She didn't need to be told. She leapt through the doorway into the alley and threw her hands ahead of her to probe the darkness, blindly continuing and expecting to hit a wall at any moment. The crackle came again, Ki's voice about to say something – and a scream hit her.

The shriek tore from the shadows, so piercing it threw her back into a wall as she cried out herself. Tova slid down, kicking, yelling, wide eyes staring up into pitch-black shadows that could contain anything or nothing at all. The scream got louder as it got closer, boring into her face.

She wrenched the VHR-38 from her ear – had forgotten it was still attached – and the sound cut out. Her chest moved with quick, deep breaths, the rest of the alley still, not even a breeze. She pulled her eyes away from the shadows, back to the alley's entrance.

The Obake thug stood in the half-light of the narrow warehouse exit, staring in alarm. Beyond him, in the empty space of the warehouse, some market stall owners had gathered, all motionless in shock. Tova's yell must have mimicked what she'd heard. No one knew how to react. But the Obake man recovered first. He took a step towards her, holding up a beefy hand warning her to stay put, and he said something. She twisted on the ground, sliding away from him. He repeated it, asking a question, demanding something – she couldn't make it out on his lips.

On the threshold of the alley, the light caught his face. He was repeating something – different words surrounding two clearly recurring sounds: *Yo say. Yo say.* He wanted her to talk?

Tova scrambled up, one hand pushing against wet brick as the other pocketed the VHR. The man moved into the shadow with her, a few steps away now. She cried out, "Get away from me!"

Her voice was met with a blinding flash of light and she threw her arms up over her face.

Plunged back into darkness, Tova blinked against the afterimage. Just inside the entrance of the passageway, the silhouette of the muscle-bound thug's legs twitched at ground level, as he struggled to gain purchase and stand again. What had she done? How?

Ki shouted, "Run!"

13

"That's it, sit right there. They do a great tea, you'll see. You're safe now. Perfectly safe. Tova? Tell me you're alright."

Tova was in a shady tenth-floor sushi bar. Hiding in a two-person booth as she stared at her hands. She'd repeated something Ki told her and the waiter had wandered away. As she rotated her hands, fingers splayed, a clay teapot was placed in the centre of the table, a small, shallow bowl in front of it. She looked up with a frown as the waiter filled the bowl with gently steaming tea. Smoky, with a hint of ginger.

The waiter ambled off without any interaction, and Tova's gaze drifted back to her hands.

"Say something, Tova," Ki said, his voice a distant blur.

When she'd said something before, her hands had *done* something. Struck that man down with lightning? The people in the market had looked at her like she was a witch. That screaming menace in the alley – had it touched her? Entered her, caused this?

"Tova, listen," Ki said. "I'm here. We made it. Dammit, *you* made it! You run like the wind, you know that?"

Could wind run? No, it was apt. Tova had never run like that in her life, blundering over obstacles – people even. She could have kept going, right out of Tokyo, across the sea. Except, without thinking, she'd come here, guided by Ki's directions.

"Are you home?" Ki continued with a playful tone. "I need you to stay with me."

"I *want* to go home," Tova announced weakly, and with the words out she felt her eyes filling. Tears. "I want to go home."

"You will, soon enough."

"Now," Tova said. "I want to go home right now. I don't want to be here. I don't..."

"It's okay. It's okay, it's over now. Honey. Darling."

Tova pulled her eyes up from her hands, past the tea, blinking back the tears. She finally took in the bar properly. There were a handful of other booths occupied, mostly men in dark suits, tables overladen with food and empty glasses. The further recesses of the room were steeped in shadow. Ki had to be closer than anyone she could see, if he could hear her.

"Sweetheart, doll –"

"I read online," Tova whispered, "about Japanese spirits. There's one that steals vegetables. When people see it, they die." She felt her voice shaking as she said it. Not joking now, not able to dismiss this. "The sight of one turned a lady purple. Killed her. A small demon, a little man, all hairy. A full-sized man couldn't hide anywhere in here. A small one might. Is that why I can't see you? You're small. You'll turn me purple?"

"The hyōsube," Ki said, with a sniff of laughter. "A silly story, it's not real."

"What *are* you, then?" Tova hissed.

A man eating at the main bar lowered his chopsticks to look her way. Too loud again. So what. Tova's hand closed around the teacup. Demons, spirits, there's no such thing...no electric fingers or screaming shadows. But there's a voice in my head. Sparks flying from my hands, screams. She whispered, "It has to be something like that. Something that means it's not *me*."

"What's not you?" Ki replied carefully.

"The mad sounds – *your* voice – shooting *lightning* from my hands!"

After a pause, Ki let out another snigger. "Oh. You tremendous beast. No. You did *not*. That was me. You've never seen a taser before? That's all it was. A high-voltage shot. No permanent damage done."

Tova glared at nothing. His flippant retort didn't ease her nerves. "You were there?"

"Yes, of course!"

"No you weren't!"

The man at the bar thumped a fist into the counter, giving her a hard stare. When Tova caught his eye, he said something bitter, maybe violent. Beyond him, the waiter who'd given her tea replied with something, telling him to relax? But watching her with concern, too. Tova looked from one to another then rested her eyes back on the tea. She'd get into other kinds of trouble if this continued. She took her phone and made a pantomime of a call. Keeping her voice studiously low, she said, "Where are you now? Where *exactly* are you?"

"You can't see me," Ki reminded her.

"In that alley," Tova said, "something screamed out of the shadows." Like it could've torn her soul in two. A sound suggesting worse fates than she could ever endure at the hands of the Obake. She added, "You were in that alley."

"All I heard," Ki replied, "was *you*. I'd say half of Tokyo heard you."

"I'm not crazy," Tova said, for herself. "I'm not."

"No, but you need to stop wearing that processor," Ki said. "That's what did it. Whatever *it* was."

"Whatever it was," Tova growled, "comes from the same place as you."

"Absolutely not," Ki assured. His tone was almost offended. "Your people have short-circuited your hearing. We're talking through a mic, not channelling spirits or something."

Your people, he said. Associating her with Mogami now? Saying she was closer to the Japanese researchers than him? She couldn't blink, not sure how she could continue without seriously challenging her own sanity.

"What can I tell you?" Ki said. "What's on your mind? Talk to Ki."

"You know what I want to know," Tova said. "Unless you're invisible, or a damned *tiny hairy man*, how can you be right here without me seeing you?"

Ki was quiet. Should she have taken her chances with Tasker? Tova said, "At least I could see the man from my government."

"No," Ki replied. "Absolutely, don't do that. He's as bad as the Obake."

"According to you –"

"I know the Obake Police and I know their equivalents."

"*How* do you know? How do you know any of that?"

"When it comes to that Ministry, I have a friend from Ordshaw. She tells me stories, when she visits. Perhaps your people are kinder, Ordshaw is more welcoming, but they are still dangerous."

"A friend from Ordshaw…" Whatever Ki was into stretched all the way back home. His infatuation with Natalie Reid had to be wrapped up in this, too.

"A client, really," Ki said thoughtfully. "She complains about Ordshaw, herself, but I see what a fantastic place it is. Certainly not as volatile as Tokyo. In truth, I am surprised your Ministry man is allowed to operate here. Did he say how he found you?"

Tova pulled herself away from thoughts of Ordshaw to consider it. She had an idea, about this Ministry picking up on something that her father must have said to the embassy, but if Ki wasn't sharing then neither would she. Besides, it was only half the story. Wasn't Tasker suspicious of Mogami already? He was at the hospital, not chasing her up in her hotel. As with the Obake men in her apartment building, there had been something going on before she'd had her operation.

"Anyway," Ki continued hastily. "You think it's a coincidence the Obake came to the hospital when you met with this guy? They were near Yoyogi Park, following a false signal Mei pinged from your phone. Something turned them around. Straight for you."

No, not straight for her. Tova had run into one of them in the subway. They didn't know exactly where she was: they couldn't have known Tasker had her waiting for a translator. More likely he had come alone, to stake out the ward, and the Obake were tipped off by her arrival. Hell. Nurse Hamada, tapping at her computer? If they could trace her messages and her passport, they'd know if her hospital record was updated...

"Ah, it is my fault." Ki kept talking. "I must apologise completely. I did not plan for everything. But we are doing our best. I can *only* apologise."

"Don't." Tova shook her head. "You can do a lot more. I want to know how you know about these people, exactly."

He said nothing. In frustration, Tova continued.

"Where are you? How did you stop that man if you weren't there?"

"I wasn't *not* there," Ki said. "Just as I'm not *not* here. Huh. Perhaps it would be best if you *did* think of the hyōsube. Some things are too dangerous to see. For everyone."

Tova gritted her teeth, wanting to throttle it out of him.

"What I did for you – they will talk about it. There will be consequences. But I couldn't let them take you. That's what friends are for, yes? Ha ha, please, tell me we're still friends?"

Biting her lip to avoid saying something too loud, Tova carefully considered her next words. Calm. Quiet. "You are the only thing in the world that I can hear, and you won't talk straight. How can we be friends if I don't even know *what* you are."

Ki was quiet again. Tova hoped he would insist she was mad

for saying something like that. Laugh it off, make a quip, *sure, Tova, you think I'm not even human?* His silence made the accusation serious.

Tova leant back. She took a slow sip of tea and found it bitter. Sat in the near-dark of an upmarket bar, close to men hunched over and talking in what appeared to be whispers. Her hearing was worse than before, her perception of reality crumbling. It wasn't supposed to be like this, not at all. Her adventure, Tova the Trooper, going it alone. Confusion over train tickets, food poisoning, *maybe*, but this? She wanted to take it all back: reset her life by a week.

Tova checked the phone in her hand. No signal, no surprise. She searched for the bar's network.

Ki said, "What are you doing?"

"What I should've done in the first place." Tova brought up her messenger app. No one online, too early. Ethan hadn't stayed up late again. She typed: *Mum. I'm thinking about getting an earlier flight back. I've had enough.* Send.

"Tova, talk to me. I want to help."

The message pinged with a cross, failed. Whatever. She'd resend it later. Tova said, "I'm going home."

"No – oh no – have hope!" Ki spoke rapidly. "You've not seen a fraction of this *Most Wonderful City*. You are safe now, that I promise – today, that was a blip, but we know what we're doing. Trust me, we will make it special again, we can do great things! There's still time for enjoyment. And the concert – a majestic experience awaits!"

"Shove your concert," she mumbled, sure it was barely audible. "You didn't hear those screams, you *don't* understand."

"Listen. Please. If you must go, I can get you a flight. One with no Obake, no Ministry. No concert, if you wish. But let me make all this up to you. Do not believe I wanted anything less than to help you. You must trust me."

Tova said nothing. Did she *ever* trust him? It seemed mad, now.

"Give me today," he hurried on. "Give me today and you can learn to love this city. You like nice food? Good sights to see? Shopping? And – yes – what about your hearing? I have the HiWave. There must be something I can do. I will make Mei move mountains for you."

"You can do something right now," Tova said. "Just explain."

"Just..." Ki faltered. No, he wasn't going to tell her a damn thing. "Give me only today. If nothing else, if your sole desire is to put this behind you, at least give me today to lift your spirits. I will leave you alone – let me only point you in the right direction."

"Alone?" Tova snapped. "You think that's the problem? Why can't you just talk to me? Properly." He didn't respond. She took a breath and continued unhappily, "You want me to trust you, but not see you, you have to tell me why. Explain what it is that makes your technology special and what you've got to do with these police."

Still silence.

"Are you listening to me?" Without an answer, Tova felt panic rising, sensing his absence. "If you'd just talk. I'll give you all the time you want, I'll even go to the concert, but you explain your part in this. Tell me something. You can't just shut up every time I ask."

That's exactly what he'd done, though. Exactly as before. As clearly as Tova sensed when he was around, she knew that he was gone. Drably, Tova recalled the same feeling at work. Chasing accounts across different council departments, dealing with people who avoided responsibility by not replying to messages. Now she had someone she could talk to, who she could hear, and it was the same fucking distancing tactic. With a grunt, she took hold of the tea bowl, wanting to pitch it across the room, maybe crack it over someone's head. Anyone's, it didn't matter who. Her movement caught the eye of the man at the bar. One more angry look from him told her if she did anything, he'd answer in kind.

She looked away, resisting, and her eyes rested on a broad-stroke painting of mountains on the far wall. Kanji lettering lining one side. Six thousand miles from home, somewhere completely different, and all she'd seen was hospitals and hotels. Faced bizarreness all of her own, instead of the exotic temples and foods the country should have offered.

But what was she supposed to do? She couldn't go back to Mogami and the hospital; people would be watching them, and if Mogami had answers they weren't sharing. Sean Tasker, she wanted to have hopes for, but couldn't for a second think him safe to talk to. Not just because of what Ki had said; she had her instincts, and there was a dangerous iciness in Tasker's face. On the flipside, she had the cheeriness of Ki's voice, lively, friendly. But she couldn't see *his* face; for all she knew Ki delivered all his merriment with a scowl. Her only sensible path was to simply abandon thoughts of all of them.

Her phone pinged with a message.

A URL, from Ki, loading with a thumbnail preview. Senso-ji, with an image of a massive pagoda. Another message followed, another URL. Tova frowned at Ginza Six. A shopping centre? Another followed, and another. He was sending suggestions of things to do? Tova scoffed, writing a response: *TALK TO ME.*

Another message popped up that gave her pause. VR Zone. An image of someone in what looked like a cockpit. An immersive virtual reality theme park? Tova's thumb hovered curiously over it. Somewhere to lose herself...

Ki sent a written message, next: *We will arrange a flight for you. Take care of everything. Only do not panic. Isn't it time you had some fun?*

Tova glowered at the words, wanting to hate him, wanting to bite back, knowing this wasn't good enough and that she should do everything possible to hunt this mystery man down and force some answers. More URLs followed, though. A noodle bar. A park. An exotic row of market stalls. All so different to anywhere Tova had been before. The fantasies her trip was supposed to contain; how she'd pictured it before coming. There had always been a chance the surgery would fail, and her plan was always to enjoy this city, regardless.

It cost her enough to come here, this was her adventure, and the damn city *owed* her.

Eyes resting on the picture of the market selling eclectic clothes and odd electric gadgets, she was caught between completely cutting off Ki and this madness and simply trying to roll with it. He'd given her a lot already – a flight wasn't out of the question, was it? At this point, with his reticence, it felt like *he* owed her. Then she could use what time she had left without worrying about the pressure she might put on everyone back home. And with Japan's prolific electronics, maybe she could find something unusual to arm herself with, in the meantime. Now Ki had planted the thought, she imagined she'd feel an awful lot better with a taser.

*

An alarm signalled on Ki's desk. He shut down the weaving machine and switched off his music, then changed channel on the HiWave to listen in on the hotel room. Tova was returning after her day out. 9pm. Good girl. Anyone exposed to Tokyo for that long had to enjoy it.

Tova tossed her shoes aside and emptied a carrier bag of shopping onto the bed. What had the darling bought? Some childish keyrings, a couple of trinkets imitating traditional charms, and – oh no. She picked up a plasticky parka jacket and stretched it in front of her, turning on the spot so Ki got a good look. Awful, just awful. Shiny, silver, pink and blue combined in jagged triangular panels, piped around the cuffs. It wasn't fitted, would hang from her shoulders like a flag. God *no*. And her smile. So proud. Ki should've given her a lot more than just socks.

Tova huddled over her tablet, propped up for a video chat, and used sign language as she showed off her purchases. Whatever she said about the parka, it made her crease with laughter. Ki could have screamed. Then came a keyring she was equally proud of; Ki squinted to make it out. Not a keyring, a miniature air horn, small enough to fit her palm, a chunky red button in the centre. Was she going to prank someone?

The phone rang and Ki flipped down the mic on his headset.

"She's back," Mei said.

"I know. You see what she bought?"

"Think it's for self-defence? I could improve it for her, actually give it some impact."

"I meant her hideous coat."

"She seems to like it," Mei said.

Ki huffed. What did Mei know – she dressed like a sewer-worker herself, no matter how many times he told her so. "Whatever. I suppose we should count ourselves lucky she's smiling at all after this morning." His tone clearly conveyed his message to Mei; they should never have let her go to the hospital, and there must have been more Mei could have done to secure it.

Mei responded defensively, "She had to try. And proving this research is now on the UK Ministry's radar? That was surely worth it."

"It's not our problem. Mogami are done with her, she's done

with them, this'll fizzle out."

"And if it doesn't? You saw the look on her face, hearing those things. This could be –"

"Her hearing the screams of something else, some kind of fiends?" Ki knew where Mei's fears would take them. It deserved a derisive laugh. "Are you a child? As bad as that *goof*. You know what she accused me of being? Hyōsube."

Mei waited a frosty moment before responding, "You think that's funny?"

"Oh come *on*, she's not serious. Even that loping fool doesn't believe in such things. She had a messed-up ear operation, not a spiritual epiphany."

"An operation that connected her to us."

"Yes, to us," Ki said. "Not some other pitiful fancy. And the Obake are here for *us*."

"What about the Englishman?"

"Ah! What does it matter?"

"If it *is* fiends," Mei answered sharply, "we might at least make sure it won't kill her."

"Don't be so dramatic. All she has to do is leave the thing off her ear." Ki spun on his chair, wondering himself how this all got so complicated. He had a solid, simple plan, which should never have involved Mei talking back, much less all the questioning demands from the *human*. He sighed. "Frankly, you were right in the first place. This interaction was a mistake. You wanted me to admit that? You were *right*. Congratulations, I'm convinced of the folly of talking to them. But it's fine, we'll cut it off once the concert's arranged. Give her *space*. You have secured the concert ticket, haven't you? Her meeting?"

Mei didn't answer.

"Mei? Tell me you did that right."

"Yes, it's ready. She was right, Mogami didn't seem prepared to go through with it, so I sent messages via their servers. But I'm not happy. Not if her implant is doing what I'm afraid of. If we get her up the Skytree, I can get some answers."

The Skytree, where the yōsei's best monitoring equipment was safe from prying eyes. The only place in the city they'd managed to stay effectively concealed.

Ki watched Tova on the monitor. Chatting away with her odd hand movements, cheerful, over the morning's drama. She'd still go to the concert, now she'd calmed down. No one would turn down that offer. They just needed to distract her long enough to get her there.

The Skytree was as good an attraction as any; it might even give them more leverage. And seeing as Mei was getting so worked up over this...Ki said, "Okay. Sure. Let's help her. Since it's so dear to you, *you* can be the one to hold her hand."

"Me?" Mei replied with shock. "You want me to talk to her?"

"Yes. You seem to forget my time is *valuable*. Test that device of hers, see what it means – if anything. Make her think she has some answers either way, but of course don't *tell* her anything. In fact...I'll tell you exactly what to say."

14

Tova leant over a rail towards a window that looked down from 600-odd metres high, Tokyo stretched out in miniature beneath her. The cloudy day rendered the city strangely colourless from this angle, a contrast to the dazzling neon of street level. The river was a mute blue channel, cars crawled the roads like ants, and the occasional patches of green only accentuated the muted whole. The circular corridor of the Tembo Galleria, atop the Skytree tower, was more or less empty; Tova's disability access had got her in ahead of a thin crowd. A chill breeze pushed in around foot level, either overzealous air-conditioning or slight cracks in the insulation.

"Hey," a small female voice said.

Tova looked up and around before settling in to the now-familiar realisation there was no one there. "Mei?"

"Yes."

"You're invisible, too, right?" Tova asked tentatively, searching the surrounding corridor. Her eyes were drawn to a shadow in a corner of the ceiling. Difficult to focus on – was there something there? Maybe a camera they could see her through?

"Not invisible," Mei said.

"And no Ki?"

"No. I will do the tests."

Not the best start. Mei's voice was clipped, the unfriendly, unwilling opposite of Ki. Tova had pushed him and he'd balked, palming her off to someone who wanted even less to do with her. Stress rising through her bones, Tova turned back to the view, searching for calm.

Mei's voice said, "Is Ordshaw similar?"

"To this?" Tova pictured the contrast. Ordshaw had its mix of modern towers in the centre and impressive churches, and Old Ordshaw had some beautifully warped medieval streets. But, to her, Ordshaw was most evocatively the neighbourhood of Ripton, characterised by terraces, smoke-blackened brickwork and overturned bins. "No. Not really."

"More friendly?"

Tova looked over her shoulder, as though the woman was right there, and saw only the empty space of the corridor. "Do you believe the same as Ki, that Ordshaw is special?"

"Do you?" Mei's tone suggested it was foolish. Tova felt her cheeks flushing. It was one of the few things she had to go on; a link between their two cities, with Natalie Reid as ambassador, might indicate who these people were. If she could sway Mei to talk...

"You don't...." Tova hesitated. "You don't sound happy to be here. Working with him."

"Really?" Mei answered without interest. "He has big ideas. Not always good ones."

"Are you –"

"Let's get on with this. You understand why you are here? Our people have technology in this tower. Hidden from Obake sensors. I will activate and deactivate a sequence of transmitters, see if any affect your hearing."

Tova stirred a foot, trying to avoid getting her hopes up. Ki's morning messages, bidding her to join him here, had said more or less the same thing. These revelations about the Skytree hardly gave her a better idea of who she was dealing with, and rather than believe they could help, Tova told herself it was worth visiting for the view, another experience ticked off while she waited to go home. She said, "You are arranging a flight for me, aren't you?"

Mei gave a little snort. Annoyance at the task, or dismissal of it? She said, "You'll fly tomorrow, at the latest. I will disable the HiWave now. Then begin my tests. Ready?"

Tova took a breath. Her hand teased the VHR-38 in her pocket, an ever-present reminder that hearing wasn't necessarily a good thing. She nodded, and Mei said, "I'll be back soon."

Dropped into silence, Tova observed the city, resisting the urge to feel hopeful. The VR Theme Park and the wacky shops she'd visited had calmed her, but not as much as the thought of home. Ki was right, at least, that one day of fun *had* helped: she could call this adventure a success, with or without her hearing. They just needed to go through the motions of these tests to confirm that *nothing could be done*, and then she could make up explanations from the safety of her one-bed on Ripton High Street. Her eyes wandered as her mind did. She focused on the ceiling again, looking for that possible camera. Gone, now.

Tova frowned. Had she imagined the shadow before? Was it cast by a passing bird?

Minutes passed as she wondered if Ordshaw was any safer than here. Given that she didn't exactly know who was chasing her or why. Was the UK outside this conspiracy's reach? When she signed in a pub, would there be Obake agents or Sean Tasker's people keeping watch? Ethan would shit himself knowing what she was into.

"Test, one-three," Mei's voice said. "One-three."

"I hear that," Tova announced, turning on the spot. There was no answer. She waited for Mei to return, but when the voice didn't come again she settled back into her thoughts.

Ethan. She'd tried to avoid thinking about him since he'd first dismissed what she was going through. It was almost surreal, holding this waking nightmare up alongside the bland thought of what to do with *him*. Ethan in his grey malaise, waiting for her to get home and settle in his crusty living room like a barnacle. That wasn't her, not any more. Not since coming here. No, since earlier – not since she went behind his back and entered Mogami's lottery, and let herself hope for something different. And now she potentially had a flight tomorrow, *at the latest*; she needed to make the most of this. The Shinjuku Deaf Club met this evening, but she could do that kind of mingling back home. She would go to the Imperial Palace, and see the Great Lanterns, both of which were probably best enjoyed without hearing anyway.

"Anything?" Mei's voice came back.

"I heard you," Tova said. "You said one-three."

"Right," Mei said, completely flat. "Anything else?"

"No," Tova shook her head.

"Okay. Stage Two. Plug your processor in."

Tova went rigid, fingers squeezing the VHR. "It's not going to work."

"You don't want to try?"

"You didn't hear what I heard."

Silence as Mei reflected. Tova's eye was drawn to two young Japanese people walking arm in arm up the corridor, giggling and pointing out of the windows. They stopped to take in the view. Mei said, a little quieter, "You are safe, and I am watching. This is the only way we can explore it."

"Mm," Tova said, looking away from the couple. Back over the shadows of the corridor – it was back. She stared. The same small dark patch where the wall met the ceiling. She took a step closer, trying to make out what it was. Checked the window, nothing casting a shadow from outside.

As Tova furrowed her brow, Mei's curt voice announced, "I'm switching off the HiWave. Plug in your processor and give me a few minutes. I assure you it's not dangerous."

Tova looked down again, to take out the VHR-38. It was easy for Mei to dismiss the screams, not having heard them. They were bone-chillingly haunting. And now Tova thought of it...this had all gone wrong after she'd first heard them. After the operation had seemed to work. What if it was those sounds that damaged her ear? How did she know they weren't dangerous? No. She closed her eyes. Hamada would've found evidence if that was at all possible. However troubling those sounds were, they couldn't hurt her.

Bracing herself, Tova clicked the VHR-38 into place.

She stayed braced a moment longer.

She opened her eyes. Nothing, again. The disappointment of silence.

She exhaled. Okay. Whatever she'd been through –

A sea of some distant sound slowly crept into Tova's ear: a deep, rumbling groan that drew her widening eyes to the city below. Moving to the window, she picked out the veins of the streets between towering buildings, knowing, somehow, that the sounds were there. The whole city humming.

"Something?" Mei's voice returned over the rumble. "What is it?"

Tova held up a hand for quiet.

At this height, surely it wasn't possible to hear the city's bustle? Was it an immense wind, channelled through the urban canyons? But any wind that strong would knock down the trees. Or at least make them sway. The sound rose and fell, a wave of creaking, moaning – no – Tova backed away from the window.

"You don't hear it, do you?" Tova said.

"What is it?" Mei repeated.

Tova closed her eyes to concentrate.

It wasn't a groan, or the wind. It wasn't one thing at all, but layer upon layer of similar sounds rolling over one another – so many, so immense, that they reached all the way to the top of this tower. Not as frightening or horrific as up close, but every bit as harrowing now she understood what they were.

The screams spread across the entire city. Every corner of every street, countless hidden sources, shrieking in anger. It had infected Tokyo in its entirety. And it brought the hints she'd been gathering from Ki to the fore – these mysterious *ghost* police, they were here, after her, because she'd connected to something *unnatural*. "What is it? How did they get here?"

Mei answered very slowly, "What can you hear?"

"Everything," Tova uttered. Then she shook her head. "Not the sounds of – not the world I can see. But every part of whatever else is down there."

She backed away from the window, turning to observe the sound rising from every direction. Not up here – thank God – all rising from ground level.

A trio of Japanese tourists came down the corridor, one with a heavy camera hanging around his neck. They were pointing and talking. As oblivious to the horror spread through the city as Tova was to whatever they were saying. Her ear was only good for cryptic voices and secret screams. She stepped out of their way, cringing as something emitted a particularly piercing shriek below, like a giant bird being crushed. She raised a hand to the VHR-38, but didn't remove it.

"How can I go back down there?" she whispered.

"We'll deactivate the transmitter –"

"What *is* it?"

Mei went quiet.

"You know. You know what I'm hearing. It's why they're hunting me – something to do with those sounds. Is it why you have to stay hidden, too? Tell me."

"I don't know."

"Tell me!" Tova had raised her voice way too loud, getting shocked looks from the three tourists. She lowered her head, a hand over her face, and said, quieter, "You have to tell me."

"I don't know," Mei repeated. Before Tova could protest again, she continued, "It is connected. It must be. But...if it is real...it's the stuff of legends."

"What legends? *Whose* legends?"

Again Mei hesitated, before replying, "Describe it to me."

"The city is screaming!" Tova hissed. "The whole city. It's coming from everywhere! Things we can't see, *screaming*. I can hear it from here!"

Mei cursed in Japanese.

"How can I –"

"Stop listening," Mei warned, quickly. "Take that thing off." Tova hesitated and Mei spoke more urgently: "Do not listen to whatever it is!"

Tova disconnected the VHR, startled by the fear in her voice. The sounds of the city cut off, as if they'd never been there. She didn't plummet into complete silence, though; she could hear Mei's frightened breathing.

15

"Ki's not answering," Mei said, "but he will call when he sees my message, I am sure."

In all her life of silence, Tova had never found it so chilling as now. Sitting on a stool at the edge of the Skytree Café, the city stretching beneath her, she longed for the comfort of Ki's friendly voice. Something to counter the memory of those colossal groans. Mei's serious tone only gave the thought more weight.

The conclusion of the experiment was clear enough: however Tova's skewed hearing worked, it was triggered by a piece of technology uniquely used by Ki and Mei's people, and the VHR-38 jumped it up a notch. Nothing they'd tested in the hospital had the same effect; it was possible no one had paired these two pieces of tech before, to say nothing of whatever the injection had done to Tova. There was every chance that she was the only person who could hear these sounds. She was alone. With all that out there.

"It can't touch you," Mei said, stiffly. "Can't hurt you."

"You don't know that, you don't understand it," Tova replied. A guess, confirmed by Mei's lack of response. "But you know what it is."

"I might...know the nature of it," Mei admitted. The concern in her tone was scarcely better than her previous hostility. "It's clear which part of our technology triggered it. I hoped it would be something else."

Tova's eyes ran back over the café. Just her and that loving couple here, sat far across the hall. The tables were slim modern ones offering nowhere for Mei to hide, unless she was thin as a chair leg. "What's special about your people? Your technology?"

"A lot," Mei said. She exhaled in a way that Tova hoped suggested she was giving in. Ready to talk. "We've developed in isolation. Quite separate to you. Whatever Mogami have done to you, these two paths were not meant to cross."

"But they did," Tova said. "Because you came for me."

"Yes." Regret, now.

"What did you mean, *separate to you*? You don't mean Westerners, do you?"

Mei didn't reply. As forthcoming as Ki.

"Mei. Tell me what this is." Tova felt the words shaking in her throat. "Please."

"Ki – he told me – what we should do –"

"I don't want his instructions. He didn't even come! *Please*, give me the truth."

The couple across the café sat up straight, startled. Tova ducked her head, trying to adjust her volume. This was no time to excite attention, get kicked out. Though maybe if she got loud enough they'd kick her out of Japan completely, send her back to Ordshaw: *we don't want this nuisance here.* Yes, please.

Mei ventured, slowly, "There's...many things the Obake conceal. Mysteries we don't know ourselves. This is the territory we've entered."

"Start with who *you* are then. The HiWave, the way this works. You know what's triggering the sounds? Isn't there a reasonable explanation?"

Mei grunted uncomfortably, then began a slow answer. "An explanation, maybe, but not a reasonable one. The HiWave uses a different kind of radio wave. Not electromagnetics, like your wireless. Energy waves untouched by your technology. For the headset, this is trivial, an alternative channel, to produce a clear sound. But the transmitter up here, the one that triggered your hearing, uses these waves like a radar. Scanning for a very particular purpose."

"Which is..." Tova dreaded the answer. The foreboding, she realised, had been there since the first screech she'd heard that night in Kabukicho. Her imagination conjured thoughts of fairy tale and fantasy because the signs were there. It *felt* real.

"This scanner picks up the activities of our people," Mei said. "And disturbances that are best avoided. When this energy shifts, bad things happen. There are anomalies, not things we have explained – they are particularly bad in Tokyo, so we stay far away. All we have are horror stories. Not everyone believes them."

Tova regarded the view with what she felt should be a different perspective. What was really down there, between the endless blocks of varying grey? "Horror stories like what? What could produce screams like that?"

"I've never heard anything like it," Mei replied quietly. "I just know its nature..."

Nothing about the way she said that sounded good. Tova said, "Couldn't it just be your weird transmitter warping the way I hear? Creating an impression of something that's not there? Why shouldn't this all be in my head? I could accept that – I know I've –"

"Does your imagination account for proximity?" Mei countered.

Tova tripped on that. She definitely had a sense of how far away the screams were. Just as she'd sensed them closing in on her in the park, or that one approaching in the alley.

"In Obaida," Mei said, "there was said to be a sea serpent that could induce paralysis through touch alone. Twice as long as a man, capable of swallowing you whole."

An anaconda? Tova frowned, thrown by the tangent. So?

"They say it glowed, between its scales. Our scanners found a disruption in the same waves as those that are affecting your hearing. Before we could investigate further, the Obake Police erased the phenomenon. A village of people disappeared with it. A sudden illness, it was reported. Many dead. The reports we have of the serpent were whispers from distant people, those who did not know enough for the Obake to silence. Now, I could not tell you for sure if there was a serpent there, or something else entirely. I can tell you the result, though. I can tell you it was dangerous."

Tova bit her lip. It was an uneasy parallel, those surrounding screams, this monstrous anecdote and the invisible voices in her head. *Your people*. The *unnatural*. The way Ki used that distinction *human*. Tasker used it, too. She asked, "What are you?"

Another long pause.

"It can't be worse than an invisible screaming horde or a magic snake."

"What do *you* think we are?"

The question took Tova by surprise. With this talk of myth and monsters, the possibilities were wide open. Except again her eyes kept searching, expecting to see Mei somewhere close by. And there were those small blemishes in the environment she couldn't quite make out. A bug, a bird, a shadow. She whispered, "Can you change your appearance? Your size?"

"Do you think we need to?" Mei said. "We have technology smaller than you'd imagine."

It was a deflection, but in it Tova suspected the truth. Mei was right that the sense of proximity was what made the screams feel real. It was the same with them. The sounds from the HiWave got distant, then louder again, when she moved around the park. Ki had been nearby, but they kept insisting they weren't invisible. *Smaller than she'd imagine* didn't have to apply to machines. Not if *they* were small. Small enough to hide in shadows. Small enough to sneak into a hospital, change her appointment. Steal a credit card, maybe a passport, to book a hotel. Make a noise above her room, not from the apartment above – somewhere in between? Small enough to manufacture socks with a material so tight it seemed out of this world? Hell, Ki had said the socks would help her understand.

Tova dragged her hands over her face, checking herself.

You're really considering this? Seriously?

Her eyes rested on the expanse of Tokyo, the screams coming back to mind. If that monstrous unseen sound was possible then anything was. She said, "Your people. The Obake want to hide you..."

"The Obake want a lot things hidden," Mei said. "Some, with good reason. Things that have been better hidden from your people than ours. We have words for them. In your language, fiends of prey. The sights that slaughter."

"Things like sea serpents?"

"Worse. Our scanners prove their existence but not what they are. Unnatural forces."

"Which Mogami gained access to? Oh my God, did they inject me with –"

"No," Mei cut in quickly. "No, I don't think so. Your hospital records show no understanding of how your hearing processor has created your situation. The missing link is somewhere in the injection they gave you, but the Obake would shut the whole company down if there had been any clear connection between that and our world. I suspect they stumbled into this, perhaps even created an artificial connection."

Tova fixated on *our world*. Not just different people, a whole other world of possibilities. Apparently policed by people more powerful than Mogami Industries, a massive multinational. "They know about *me*, though," she said. "They came hunting for me. Hearing these screams, it must mean something they understand."

Mei took her time answering. "If they know what the screams are, they don't want other people knowing. If they don't, their access to that knowledge could only make things worse."

"And what about the Ministry? The man who came –"

"A different organisation, playing the same game. Listen, you coming here, clearly connecting your hearing to our transmitter, tells us the nature of what you heard, but also that it is *down there*. Part of this city. You can get away from it. Avoid using your processor and it ends there."

"And do nothing? You have this technology – there must be something –"

Mei made a noise of either disappointment or anger, Tova wasn't sure. Her unseen companion didn't elaborate.

"There *is* something else," Tova decided. "What?"

"It might be nothing, I do not think it is the best idea," Mei said, reluctantly. "Ki wanted me to share it with you. If this turned out to be...what it looked like. I advise against it, I think you should forget all of this. Never say our names, never search for us. To ask more could open doors we cannot close."

"Tell me the idea," Tova insisted.

"The reason we involved you in the first place, it was not Ki's simple celebrity crush."

Tova frowned. So it came back to Natalie Reid...

"Ki is obsessed with your city for a good reason. It is possible that people in Ordshaw have connected with our people, recently. Their progress inspired him. Us. We wish to make progress here, too, but it is more difficult. The coming of Natalie Reid, it was an opportunity. Not just because she is from Ordshaw. There are different types of people out there. She has an energy all of her own. Warps this same energy that your hearing now does. She is not connected to the Obake, or the Ministry. She *might* be connected to something else. Our aim was to make a simple connection – to send you with a gift that might help her...open up to us."

Tova stewed, picturing the pop star's face everywhere. Swelling hearts, inspiring conversation – *devotion*. Even so. "She's just a singer."

"Yes." Mei sighed, then unhappily continued, "No. She is something more. Making this connection is not without a risk. It is possible the Obake are watching, and you have to be aware that whatever you're hearing, pursuing it further could make it worse."

And not pursuing it? Tova thought. The alternative was to wait this out, hiding, surrounded by whatever made those screams, everywhere she went. She said, "What about testing more of your technology? If your transmitter causes this, are there ways...something you could do..."

"If there was," Mei said, "we would draw my people's attention as well as the Obake's. Natalie Reid, though, is outside this realm. From Ordshaw, not Japan; an entertainer, not part of our struggle. These screams, what we might call the fiends, they are forces of inexplicable bad. She, I'd like to believe, is the opposite."

Unsure what could be the opposite of unseen creatures screaming hatefully from every corner of the city, Tova hummed at the idea. She said, "It doesn't matter anyway, Mogami never arranged my tickets."

"I did," Mei said. "They laid the groundwork, I followed through, in Valentina Joyce's name. You can go, without Mogami or the Obake knowing about it. You will be safe there."

Tova paused again. Another great adventure. She said, "What is it you think she can do for me? Or you?"

Mei took her time. Preparing just the right answer. "In both cases, we want the same thing. We have had no such contact before, we cannot say where it will go, but we have one hope. We think she will understand us."

16

Ethan signed, "You don't look good. Are you having a bad reaction to the surgery?"

As Tova went through the room picking up clothes, the video chat screen propped up on the counter, she sensed the skin under her eyes sagging from nervous exhaustion. It was bound to worry Ethan, which was the main reason she was busying herself tidying away clothes. She signed back, "Busy day, that's all. It's okay. I'm enjoying myself."

"Like hell."

"I went up the Skytree today. I'm going to the Imperial Palace soon. It's amazing here."

"Sure." Ethan's face showed how convinced he was.

Tova flashed him a smile and folded a t-shirt as he watched. She'd pack everything before the concert. Be ready to flee, whatever happened. She had hoped to find Ren online, so she might share her plan, and gain some extra enthusiasm for seeing Natalie Reid, maybe even unload about the screams and the various men chasing her. And the possibility of tiny people. But Ren wasn't around, and likely wouldn't be until late, if not until tomorrow, so all she had was Ethan telling her how bad she looked.

Ethan signed something that Tova missed. He repeated it, agitated: "Are you going to the Shinjuku Deaf Club?"

Tova shook her head. She signed, "I'm in a different part of town now."

"So? They'll be expecting you."

Tova shrugged before folding more clothes.

Ethan worriedly rearticulated his questions, drawing her attention again. "Are you okay? What's up with you? You're not even looking at me!"

"Nothing," Tova signed back. "I'm tired. I'd rather be alone."

"That's stupid!" Ethan signed animatedly. "You need support."

Tova gave him a glower. As if he had the first idea what she needed.

"I'm serious," Ethan kept signing. "The club can help you until you come back. Otherwise you'll only work yourself up. Are you trying to make things worse?"

She paused, considering Mei's same point: asking questions risked making those screams worse. It was easier to stay in a bubble, not push it. The story of Ethan's life. Hell, the story of her life before coming out here. After a thought, Tova casually signed, "Fuck off, Ethan, I can take care of myself."

Ethan froze. It took him a second to process, then his expression shifted to a satisfied smile. He signed, "You're tired. It's been tough, I'm sorry it didn't work out – but you tried, didn't you? It'll be good to have you back. We'll get everything back to normal, don't worry."

He didn't even take her insult seriously. Tova imagined the screams around his smugly smiling face. She'd waded through monsters in the park. She'd survived the chase through the market. Talked her way past Sean Tasker and spoken with whatever Ki and Mei were. Fairies or something? That's what she wanted to say – she hadn't even dared think it yet. Hell yes, why not, she'd been talking with fucking fairies. And now she was going to *meet* Natalie Reid – one of the best-known people *alive* – and she was going alone. With Ethan's simpering invitation back to their *normal* life, watching dull crime dramas on his beat-up sofa as he complained about what, the temperature of tap water?

She signed with short, piercing movements, "Stick your normal life up your arse."

He kept smiling, disbelieving, mind ticking over how to rationalise this one, as she ended the call.

Considering the horror of her morning's encounters, Tova suddenly felt lighter. She would fly home with no added hearing, but things *would* change. She was going to meet Natalie Reid, and however fucked up the world was, she was going to move forward.

By the time Tova was ready to leave for the concert, she still hadn't heard from Ki. Mei assured her they'd already contacted Natalie Reid's manager and arranged a brief backstage meeting before the show. All they asked was that Tova deliver Ki's gift – otherwise she'd be free to engage with Natalie as she pleased, though discreetly, please. No need for names. No need for specifics. She'd be going as Valentina Joyce, and she'd have no backup anywhere near the Tokyo Dome. Presumably, Tova thought, the Obake Police had monitoring equipment specifically for Ki's little people.

She really wished they'd show themselves to her. What did they look like? Maybe there was some way she could work back to it, get some leverage from this meeting...Then, maybe Natalie could offer some insight herself. They didn't know what she knew, after all.

In the hotel reception, Tova was given a package containing a plane ticket for the next day, a VIP pass to Natalie Reid's concert, and printed instructions detailing how to get to the Tokyo Dome. There was also a velvety burgundy box with a note on top: *For Natalie.* Tied with ribbon and sealed with a metallic sticker, so Tova couldn't peek inside. It wasn't heavy, perhaps more clothing? That could be an impressive enough opener, to precede a letter or something. She had on the socks again – they didn't smell yet, and were just *so good* – and felt bad for combining them with her new parka coat. But practicality won there: the coat had hefty enough pockets to fit all her essentials (passport, notebook, even the dinky air horn she'd found), meaning she wouldn't need a bag. The car crash of colours amused her, as she suspected it might amuse Natalie Reid, and the burgundy box fit in another of the coat's many pockets, so Game Tova.

At the hotel exit, she paused. Looking through the glass of the door, the peaceful street beyond, she couldn't help recalling the screams. Were they out there, right now? Waiting, around her at all times? Around *everyone*, throughout the city?

Without Ki's interference, Tova knew the VHR should transmit nothing. It might as well not exist, that parallel world of shrieking terror. She had walked through busy metro stations and shopping centres and over impossibly fast-moving roads, none of it affected by what lay unheard. But she still knew it was all *there*. Was the world itself screaming? In their fury, those sounds could have been anything – human, animal, demon? Was it the pain in the trees? The ground being trodden on? And would Natalie Reid really have a clue about that? Probably not. Maybe some way to cope, though? Some peripheral, hapless understanding?

Tova took her phone back out, delaying leaving. Think positive; if there were things out there that bad, there was good, too, wasn't there? Natalie was good. Somehow. What about Ki's people? Deceptive, maybe, but supportive of her. Tova dismissed a message from Ethan and brought up her internet browser, still open on the last thing she'd searched.

Japanese fairies.

The word for them here was *yōsei*, and the trope seemed pretty much the same as in England. Little people, with one branch specifically connected to the north, near Mount Rishiri, so that was something. She hadn't found anything else especially enlightening; the stories were limited in contrast to Japan's unique ghosts and demons, suggesting they'd scarcely captured the national imagination. But of course, if fairies existed they'd know how to stay hidden, and might manipulate whatever humans understood of them.

If fairies existed.

Tova forced a smile, looking out onto the empty street once more. There were two ways to look at it, weren't there? These were the silly fears of someone who *really* shouldn't have been travelling alone. Or she'd stumbled onto a whole new world, which so far had failed to kill her, and had tenuously put her on a path to meet Natalie Reid. She pushed the fears down, and took a deep breath, then stepped out of the building. The street was perfectly still, no one moving nearby, no vehicles. No screams.

No screams anywhere near here.

She started walking. She had time to walk all the way to the Dome, and was determined now to face this unseen horror.

After a few blocks, at a main road, where great flowering trees overhung the canal, she paused, feeling her pulse quickening. Walking too fast, trying to get away even if she told herself there was nothing here. Because there was something here, wasn't there? Behind that tree. Under the water...*something* was screaming, she just couldn't hear it. No one could. Tova squeezed her eyes shut and when she opened them again spotted a stern-faced businesswoman with a childish cat-shaped backpack. An odd clash of sincerity and cartoon. Okay. The world wasn't so bad. If there were fairies, then what else? She took a mental photo for Ren, and annotated it in her mind. Hi Mrs Cat Bag, how do you do? Quite well indeed, thank you, just on my way to Whisker Court, to present fish market analyses.

Beyond the businesswoman, a truck rolled into view, sided

with tall digital panels displaying Natalie Reid's face; moody, behind big round sunglasses. Electric text above and below announced the concert. Mrs Cat Bag turned to watch the truck pass, clearly drawn to it by shouted pronouncements, like an old world town-crier. For everything else that was strange here, Reid's familiar image fit in. There *was* something special about her. Tova couldn't wait to see how she might help.

The Tokyo Dome was the sort of venue Tova imagined they might build in space: a vast curved structure, spectacularly lit with dazzling green lettering, yellow pinpoints and a roof outlined in neon blue. Here, the high-rises played second fiddle to a ferris wheel and rollercoaster, both equally brightly lit and in full motion. Tova huddled up in her parka, buffeted by the movements of the crowd surging towards the entrances like a swarm of bees.

This was it. Show time. Literally.

Ha.

The instructions guided her towards a VIP entrance, which was perfect, because the crowd was impossibly vast. There were young, excited Asians everywhere, wearing brightly coloured plastics and leathers, outrageous sunglasses, and novelty backpacks. It made her feel better about her parka. A couple of hand-painted banners rose above the crowd, some in English: *We luv U Natalie!* and *Shibuya Reiders!*

Tova nudged her way through the shoulder-to-shoulder traffic up to the VIP gate, towards the roughly frisking Japanese bouncers – for once, locals much bigger than her. She braced herself, but when they saw her the bouncers stepped aside and bowed politely. One gave the bulges of her coat a cursory glance, but didn't touch her, assuming there was zero chance she was a threat. The virtue of being white, she mused; didn't even need a disability badge here. Moving on unmolested, she met a few onlookers' eyes and mentally pleaded for them not to hate her. Some clearly did.

A man in a suit spotted her pass and checked her name against a list. He lit up with realisation. He waved for Tova to follow and pushed his way towards a small door, flanked by more bouncers. Tova offered more queueing fans her apologetic smile as she followed. She was led through a series of corridors, the building getting darker and tighter the further they went. The suited escort reached a final door and stopped, indicating this was the end of their journey. He bowed and stepped aside. Tova gave a slight bow herself and went in.

Time to discover what business she had meeting with one of the world's most sought-after pop stars.

17

Tova sat with her knees close together in a wide dressing room, hands clasped on her lap. The smell of sweat and old alcohol rode little gusts of air that teased her hair as people darted around her. The sunken sofa sat between racks of outlandish clothing, so she watched the wall of mirrors ahead to warn her of the room's activity. A stocky red-suited Westerner was evidently in charge: Natalie's manager, pointing an authoritarian finger and rapidly telling everyone what to do. He'd introduced himself too quickly for Tova to understand, and he now had a chain of apparently incompetent people to get in line, from technicians trailing wires through to scantily dressed backup dancers or singers or whatever. No one gave a damn about Tova.

Then, as one, everyone turned reverently towards a doorway. The red suit's panic deflated, and the slump of a dozen shoulders and the widening of doe-like eyes indicated widespread, awe-filled hush.

Natalie Reid had arrived.

The star smiled into the centre of the room, wearing a scrappy white tank top and tatty khaki shorts, issuing a few soft instructions of her own. Then she was standing over Tova, explaining something to her manager. She was much smaller than Tova had imagined, perhaps a foot shorter than herself, with thin arms, but her presence filled the room. Her eyes, though dark, sparkled in the dim light, and her scent – weirdly agreeably musky – overrode the room's stagnant odour.

Tova tensed when the singer spotted her. Everyone motionless, watching, waiting for their ration of attention, and Tova felt the significance. She read Natalie's thin lips: "My God, is this her?"

Her manager was saying something but Tova couldn't break Natalie's gaze to see what. The star waved a hand to chastise him. Her eyes ran with wonder over Tova's face, picking out the marks of her scar, her shaved patch, then moved down to her garish coat.

Natalie started flapping her hands more generally, mouth wider as she shooed everyone away.

Tova twisted in her seat as the entourage was hurried out of the room. The manager was the last to go, protesting, and Natalie drove him away with a playful kick to his rear. She slammed the door behind him, laughing. A moment later, Tova almost sprang from the sofa as Natalie pounced onto it next to her, her expression like a cat with a mouse.

Tova checked to make sure they really were alone. She wasn't imagining this. She hadn't expected to have much time with the star, and now it was just them and Natalie's eager look was intimidating. *Come closer, Tova, be my blood sacrifice for tonight...*

Tova flinched when Natalie lightly tapped her thigh. Crap crap crap what was this, what was she thinking. She had no business being anywhere near this woman.

Natalie waved a hand in front of her chest, *hello*, and did a right-handed thumbs up and waved both hands near her face, a close enough attempt at *good evening*. Smiling encouragingly all the time. She then ran a thumb under her own chin, with a look of intense concentration, as Tova shifted back in alarm – a cutthroat gesture?! When Natalie tapped her two index fingers together, it became clearer she was trying to sign *nice to meet you*.

Tova exhaled relief, which the pop star noticed.

"YouTube," Natalie said, followed by a quick sentence of apology.

"Um," Tova replied uncertainly, thinking she should be the one to apologise. There was something humbling about wasting a global star's time this way, with tens of thousands of fans waiting. Natalie mouthed, naturally, nice and clear: "You can lip read?"

Tova nodded.

"Thank fuck." Natalie blew out a breath. She pointed to the door, and started speaking more rapidly, in a rant that seemed to be directed at her absent manager. Complaining, it seemed, that they weren't prepared. No translator. Natalie's face betrayed worry of her own, and one sentence seemed clear enough: "I'm more nervous than you, right?"

Tova shook her head. That seemed unlikely.

Natalie's crooked smile came back. She shrugged with her whole body. She started apologising again, and then apologised for that, having said something else she deemed inappropriate – the word *sound?* The words weren't important; her whole face spoke for her, cheeks bulging, nose crinkling; there was something impossibly likable about how expressive she was. Something uplifting about merely being close to her: Mei's talk of energy didn't seem anywhere near as esoteric faced with this woman's presence.

She was talking about the operation now; she'd heard all about Tova's tragic tale. Felt guilty herself, for some reason. The star's closing comments came out slower, easier to interpret: "And you're alone? What in actual hell, I need your story."

The star looked deep into Tova's eyes.

"Um," Tova said again. She cleared her throat. Her story. That would be something.

"You've gotta share," Natalie pressed, Tova concentrating hard on her lips. "I never even knew I had deaf fans –" She caught herself, a hand to her mouth. "Is that right? Hearing impaired? Something else?"

"Deaf is fine." Tova smiled uncomfortably, just happy that she was able to follow the young woman's rapid chain of thought. It was usually hard to pick up much of a conversation without knowing a person better, but Natalie's enthusiastic nature made the words clear.

Natalie said something else, with a friendly tap on Tova's arm, encouraging her to open up or be best mates or something. Tova shook herself out of the star's gaze and fumbled with her big pockets. Back to the plan – start with Ki's gift, then the questions. She said, "I have something –"

Natalie's knee brushed Tova's, and the star said something she didn't read. Tova took out Ki's boxed gift, and held it out hopefully. Natalie screwed up her face, then placed the box on the sofa beside them. "That's sweet – you didn't need to."

"Please." Tova gestured to the box. She needed to see it opened for herself. From Natalie's reaction to this gift, more possibilities would stem. Natalie gave her a sympathetic look.

"Sorry. That was rude."

"It's special," Tova told her, and Natalie took up the box again. She ran her hands over it – slender fingers, shining blue nails – and seemed impressed. She opened the box and navigated a nest of silken tissue paper, then drew out the contents.

Natalie held up a dark t-shirt, textured like impossibly smooth leather. She turned it over, the black material shimmering with other colours in the light, purples, emerald greens, like a crow's feathers. From the way Natalie touched the material, Tova could see how far above the socks it was. The star's finger traced the only discernible mark on the shirt, an emblem on the chest.

Natalie met Tova's eye questioningly, and Tova said nothing. Without warning, Natalie tore off the ragged top she was wearing and Tova turned away, startled. A moment of struggling later, the star had Ki's t-shirt on. Tova slowly drew her eyes back to watch the reaction. Natalie's mouth was agape as she raised and rotated her arms, testing the movement. Tova found herself staring. She knew the feeling from trying on the socks. This t-shirt, similarly seamless and incredibly form-fitting, appeared infinitely more majestic. Natalie's face said it felt even better than it looked.

Whatever else was going on, Ki's people could make clothes.

"This is..." Natalie stretched the shirt out in front of her. "...the *shit*." She turned grinning to Tova. "*Wow*."

"A gift," Tova said.

"From *where*?"

Tova smiled, wondering if Natalie would make a connection herself. At least suspect it came from an otherworldly origin. There had to be a way, after all, that this would promote Ki's people. Tova picked up the box and checked inside for an accompanying note. A few words of encouragement, contact details, a letter exploring how Natalie was special or something, why not. There was nothing, though. And though the top itself had pleased Natalie, it wasn't exactly inspiring her towards revelations of hidden powers.

With Natalie scanning the shirt up and down again, Tova's eye was drawn back to the emblem on her chest. The star caught her staring and looked too. A K and a Z, interwoven. Natalie bent around, pulling the collar up in front of her face, trying to look for the label inside. She was saying something, wondering what make the top was, and though there was no label Tova noticed a URL, woven subtly into the collar. Kzfashion.co.jp. It wasn't just the work of Ki's people – he'd made this himself, hadn't he?

"You see any other marking?" Natalie turned to her. "I love it – I'll wear it today." Tova narrowed her eyes at the next few sentences, realising the star was explaining, with gestures at the racks, that her wardrobe was usually prepared in advance – "What to wear in Tokyo, Boston, to dinner next month!" – but she'd make an exception for this – correction, *for her*.

Tova hesitated, a realisation dawning on her. This clothing was Ki's brand. That URL would point to a shop, not a hidden message, not a way for Natalie Reid to share what made her special. Well, no, it *was* a way to use her talents. Her energy wasn't magic, it was called charisma. This wasn't about the Obake or whatever parts of Ki's technology had led Tova to hearing horrors.

This was a fucking promotion.

What a catastrophic line of bullshit – *this* was what Ki wanted? To get his product in the hands of a superstar? Everything Tova had been through – maybe even the whole disaster with her hearing – was because he'd schemed to use her to persuade a pop star to wear his label?

Hey, Mr Tailor, how do you do? Quite well indeed, now I've drawn a crippled girl into a nightmare to make a name for myself.

Tova felt it bubbling up inside her. Anger. Shame.

It wasn't all lies – she was sure of that. Those screams were real, the weirdness with her hearing *was real*. Mei's fear and concern, that was real too, she was sure. Ki hadn't even manipulated her, especially; they'd said the plan was innocent, and if the surgery had simply worked she might never have known about all this parallel madness. But all along, Ki had let her believe that whatever kept him in hiding, and however he understood the Obake, meant they were in this together. He'd been placating her the whole time, not to help her resolve her situation, but to make sure she came here.

She *was* alone with those city-wide screams, and Mei was right. The only thing she could do was run, because otherwise it was her against a whole dangerous, misunderstood world.

Tova gagged, and tears rushed to her eyes. She covered her face but it was too late. Natalie stiffened and she saw the star's mouth moving through her fingers. A gentle hand on her shoulder. Tova tried to keep the sob down but her body convulsed. No, she'd come here alone – been through all this, not given in, not broken down, she wouldn't now. But she felt some sound come out of her mouth and that was it; she caved forward, shuddering as the tears flowed.

Natalie Reid squeezed her, arms around her, nose brushing against her hair. Tova felt the gentle breath of the star's uselessly whispered words entering her useless ear. She sniffed and sat back, defiantly, but Natalie kept her hands on Tova's shoulders, keeping eye contact.

"What's up?" Natalie asked simply. Earnestly.

Tova wiped another tear away. The woman before her felt impossibly familiar, like they'd known each other forever. She desperately wanted to believe in this star's magic, some ability to help. But it was because Natalie's face was everywhere, wasn't it? In truth, she was a random woman with nothing to do with this.

Natalie kept staring, waiting, until a door opened and she irritably snapped something, waving the interruption away. She turned back to Tova and said, "We've plenty of time. Look..." Her expression changed as she looked down at the t-shirt. Guilty, now. She said something about its cost.

Looking at the shirt herself, Tova considered ruining Ki's plan, tell Natalie it's from a sweatshop or she found it in the jaws of a rabid dog or something. But why? Selfish as Ki and Mei had been, it was her own damned fault she thought they could do anything. She'd convinced herself of these fantasies, that she might hear again, that invisible voices might help her. And fairies? Seriously, how could she believe that?

Tova looked up at Natalie and saw that stirring more trouble now would only make this situation worse. Ruin the one positive connection she might've made on this trip.

"Please," Tova found herself saying. "Enjoy it."

Natalie paused. "I will – I love it. But you didn't need to." Then a sentence that looked like, "I'm supposed to be helping *you*."

And of course, back to the streets of Ordshaw and Tova's dysfunctional, underachieving life. She was a charity case for this star. Some poor unfortunate in need of a hug, lucky enough to get an audience with Santa.

"It's fucking awful what happened." Natalie twisted slightly away, continuing too fast for Tova to read, bar the occasional curse and words that suggested she was discussing Mogami or the hospital. Eventually she slowed down. "I'm so sorry you're not – it didn't –" She took a moment. "I'm sorry things aren't different."

Tova said nothing. There was nothing left to say. She was utterly alone. As far from home as she could be. A fool.

"It hit me, Valentina." The singer's hand found hers. Tova barely watched her lips, catching the sense of what she was saying easily enough: something about how much her fans meant to her. The hardships they went through, and how much she wished she could do more. How unjust it felt. Tova nodded along.

Natalie rolled her head back, looking to the ceiling in a prayer of curses Tova couldn't make out. She caught a phrase, as the star looked down, "An Ordshaw girl."

They held eye contact again, and Tova saw some sadness there. She appreciated, at least, that they had that between them. Coming from a shared background *did* mean something to Natalie, as Ki had predicted.

Hey, Natalie Reid, how do you do? I miss my home, just like you.

Continuing her chain of thought, Natalie's lips read, "You grew up in Ordshaw?"

Tova nodded. "Ripton."

"You live there now?"

Another nod.

"We could've passed each other in the street." The star's smile came back, and a short diatribe followed, expressing sympathy, that Natalie understood this meeting was special to Tova – that it was special to her, too. Then back to frustration, wishing there was something she could do. "Is there anything at all?"

Tova wasn't sure how best to respond, and she was sure her unplanned response came out bitterly: "You don't believe you're magic, do you?"

Natalie paused like she wanted to get the joke. It was clear enough that something special, the unnatural, hadn't touched Natalie in the same way it had her. The star's smile faded. She shifted closer again, disregarding any sense of personal space, reading Tova's face as if studying artwork. When she spoke, she was too close for Tova to read it, and when she sat back again Tova raised a questioning eyebrow.

"What have you been through?" Natalie asked, the question clear on her face.

Hey, Tova Nokes, how do you do?

Not so well, indeed. Let me tell you.

Without giving it any more thought, Tova said, "The implant, it exposed me to some bad stuff. I'm ready to go home."

Natalie's hand was back on Tova's shoulder. This, it seemed, she could work with. "Well, you're still here now, so let's make that count." And the meaning of the next few words came to Tova perfectly, like they were meant just for her. "We'll give you something good to take back to Ordshaw, and Tokyo can keep the rest."

When Natalie's entourage returned, Harry the manager was flustered, almost angry. Behind him half a dozen dancers and a technician were vying for space to get through the doorway. Natalie waved her hands as she tried to calm them. They were coming in anyway. How long had they been waiting? Had they been listening? It didn't matter; Tova's time was up and the chaos of the show was pressing in. She got up, straightening out her clothes, and prepared to leave under the watchful eyes of a group of jealous dancers.

Natalie came back to her, put an arm around her shoulders, and spoke into her face, too close to have any chance of reading. Then she sprang away, as Surly Harry gave Tova the eye. Tova stood in confusion for a few moments, the action around her quickening, before Natalie reappeared and insisted, clearly this time, "It's not a hello and fuck off deal, okay? Enjoy the show, Valentina."

Tova smiled back. Making friends with a superstar was something, wasn't it? With one minor problem – as Natalie turned away, Tova called out, "That's not my name –"

It had no impact, Natalie talking to someone else, crew bustling into the way. Tova spoke up. "My name's Tova. Tova Nokes."

The room was still, everyone looking at her with the familiar stunned look that told her she'd overcompensated. Harry looked especially suspicious, and Natalie a little confused. But the star shrugged off the declaration and held up a thumb. Fine with her. The room erupted into movement again, the deaf girl forgotten.

18

Meeting the star, followed by Natalie Reid's immense performance, was an antidote Tova never could have guessed would work. The attention of someone of such stature was warming on its own, but there was something so genuine and caring about her that Tova couldn't help wondering if there was some truth in Mei's claims after all. Natalie had a magic all of her own, and knowing her could help Tova, one way or another. It was written in the sheer scale of the excited crowd, all there for Natalie. The stadium's vibrations rumbled through Tova as she stood stage-side with a perfect view of tens of thousands of eager faces. Their euphoria went beyond happiness. Not sure what to do faced with the possibility of being *this close* to Natalie Reid, some simply screamed. Tova saw this army of fans, with their unbridled enthusiasm, pushing back against the secret screams, the ones they couldn't hear. And this person that they all loved, and craved, had offered her support to Tova. Tova was part of this, however little she belonged there.

When Natalie strode purposefully past Tova, into a swarm of warm-up dancers, with a pat on Tova's arm, Tova shared the crowd's ecstasy. The stage shook under her feet, the music thumping through her from the enormous speakers, and Tova felt embraced. She picked out Natalie's voice in the vibrations. The stage lit up in bold flashes, pyrotechnics burst across the front, and the crowd moved as one, jumping and waving like grass in a field. It was almost possible to forget all she'd learnt. The power of this moment, could it drive off the horrors they couldn't see or hear? If the city was screaming, these people were screaming back. Protecting Natalie, themselves, *her*.

In the middle of the stage, and up a long gangway that took her out amongst them, Natalie moved fast, bouncing alternately from a dancing walk to a crouch, microphone in one hand, the other reaching towards her audience. A big man was crying in front of the stage, overcome with joy. Ki's t-shirt danced with her, subtly picking up the lighting, stunning in its simplicity. And Tova hung on to Natalie's words. She'd have something good to take back, for sure.

Tokyo *could* keep the rest.

All she needed to do was leave. However selfish his plans proved, Ki had delivered her to a fine hotel and they had provided her with a return flight. She'd be on her way home tomorrow, and she never needed think of Mogami or the VHR or the Obake Police again. She had been happy before she came to Japan and she'd be happy when she got back. *Happier*, now she'd met a superstar – and got the guts to move on.

Tova was beaming with delight, bouncing on her feet, by the time Natalie finished her first song and marched back towards her. The speakers vibrated with the star's voice, addressing the crowd – they moved with uproarious applause – then Natalie pointed to the wings, to Tova. Tova froze, feeling the eyes of half the world on her. Natalie turned away again, that little announcement done, but a great number of people were still looking her way – cheering, jumping up and down.

Whatever Natalie had said, it moved *thousands* of people, all at once.

And the star burst into another song.

Something touched Tova's arm and she looked sideways at the reassuring face of one of the backup dancers, taking a breather between songs. The girl shouted something that Tova didn't read. Either that she was *so brave* or maybe *you rave?* Tova smiled back.

She trusted it wasn't pity and sadness people were offering.

They were saying *good on you.*

You're one of us.

Ki watched the broadcast with his arms folded, Mei standing by his side with one hand on a holstered pistol. The restless scene at the Tokyo Dome had gone dark in anticipation of the concert starting, as they silently waited to see the star. Not that there was much conversation to be had: Mei had been increasingly quiet right from when Tova started hearing those screams. It suited Ki fine, he didn't especially want her theories – nor could he stand much more of Mei's pessimism. They had manoeuvred that masterpiece of clothing right into the lap of Natalie Reid, and all

Mei did was fill the room with stuffy complaint.

The stage lit up, and the music and dancing started, and Ki saw his t-shirt on display. It was enough to push all thought of Mei far away. He grinned so hard it could have reached his ears. That beautiful, goofy girl had done it. Tova had over-delivered: the diva was wearing it *tonight*.

As Natalie Reid pranced across the stage, the cameras picked her up from different angles. The fitted fabric moved like symbiotic flesh. Mei shifted on her feet, even her iciness thawed by the sight.

"Look, look!" Ki pointed. The camera was holding on Natalie's upper half, her face, the KZ logo clear on her chest. A screenshot worthy of a poster. Ki's hands were over his mouth. "We did it."

"She did it," Mei corrected, not quite with him.

"Oh, could you show a shred of enthusiasm? Watch the website – you watch the website, demand will be coming in –" Ki twisted away from the screen then caught himself, stopped, looked back at the performance. Well, the logo wasn't enough. Reid would explore the site herself later, talk about it in interviews. *I found them by chance – these people make the most amazing clothes.* She would, she definitely would, because people would ask after seeing this. "Did you ever think a human could look so good?"

"Mm," Mei grunted back. Not denying it, at least.

It was just the beginning. There were the shorts, the shoes to replace. Ki might even advise her on her hair, if Natalie's people opened a line of communication. They *had* to, didn't they? And the Obake couldn't stop it – to cross someone of her celebrity would risk huge exposure – they had to concede allowing these clothes out into the world. It would work because it wasn't electronics, or anything else identifiably yōsei; just honest, *excellent* handmade clothes. Ki would be keeping everything about his operation secret, mysterious, and that would appease the Obake, and Mount Rishiri. But it would spread all the same. It wouldn't just be Ordshaw creating waves.

"A revolution's coming," Ki said, almost giddy. "With KZ Fashion leading the charge."

"Congratulations," Mei replied flatly.

"I'm not letting you ruin this," Ki said, laughing her off. There had to be fifty thousand in the Dome, and they'd all go away dreaming of that top. "You're part of this, too, Mei. Enjoy it."

"It seems less important now," Mei muttered, tripping Ki's humour at last.

"No?" he snapped back, straightening up again. "Demonstrating the value of our talents is unimportant? Demonstrating we have more culture, more class, more demand than *them*? That doesn't seem so important, in the face of a girl hearing things that don't exist?"

"They do exist," Mei snarled.

"If you can't see it, and you can't hear it, why believe it? You'll see, she'll get over it all. Go back to her dull life with an amazing story to tell."

Natalie Reid wound down the first song and started talking to the crowd, trotting towards the edge of the stage. "I'm so thrilled to be here, Tokyo – you sure know how to show a classless girl from Ordshaw love!" The camera panned, picking out people in the wings. There was Tova! Ki pointed excitedly at the sweet dork amid the beautiful people. And Natalie was talking about *her*.

"– an extra special guest from my home town. Gave me this amazing top." Natalie indicated the t-shirt. "She went through a lot coming to your city, Tokyo!" Reid made that word work for her, the crowd erupting. "My new friend, a beautiful soul, Tova Nokes!"

The cheering escalated to a frenzied roar; they'd go mad for her shopping list if she gave it. But she'd given much more than that. Ki's cheeks were aglow.

"Did you hear that?" Mei said.

"You bet I did," Ki laughed. "The top gets a mention *and* the girl's happy. Surely you –"

"She said her name." Mei stilled him with a severe look. Ki's smile was gone. "She just said Tova's name. Her real name. Live on TV."

As the next song started, Ki stayed quiet, Mei's stare boring into the side of his head, imploring a reaction. He wouldn't give in to it. They were exactly where they'd intended to be, the best result possible. Tova was happy, Natalie was happy, what difference did a name make, now? He said, "What do you think would be best next – shorts?"

Mei opened her mouth to say something, but he cut her off.

"Don't ruin this, Mei, knowing full well there's nothing more you can do."

And she went quiet, exactly as Ki knew she would. Sure, she would pout, complain, act the martyr. She'd take her theories back to Mount Rishiri, once the rest of the yōsei got over the audacity of what they'd done, and she'd stir up a fuss with her friends in research and scanning, but she'd get over it. She'd accept the wealth this brought both of them, distract herself with the thrill of keeping their operation hidden. They had more than enough on their plate without risking anything more for a human.

It wasn't *their* fault she'd stumbled into the path of monsters.

When the show finished, Natalie Reid shot triumphantly past Tova, out of sight, to make sure everyone knew it was over. The crowd were clapping with such fervour that the huge speakers were shaking in their brackets. The stage bounced from the stamping of feet. The vibrations became rhythmic, the whole world joined in a chant for an encore.

Tova clapped. Only as the music stopped did she realise she'd lost herself in it. The beat, and the movement all around her, had drawn her in like a trance. She didn't hear what they heard, but she felt it. Deep down, somehow, she understood the feeling behind the songs. And she wanted more, as everyone else did. She shouted it.

Natalie let them wait, driving the crowd to the point of madness when she came back, and Tova found herself impossibly proud. One of her own, out of Ordshaw, capable of all this. When the star raced back to the stage, Tova fought the urge to reach out and touch her. Natalie gave her a wink on the way. The speakers shook once again with her voice, the star introducing another song.

Tova soaked it up.

As the next song thundered on, she scanned the vast crowd. There'd be a crush to get away from the stage when all this finished. She could slip out now, head back to the dressing room and wait without being crushed underfoot. As Natalie continued into a longer encore, Tova slowly peeled herself away, back down the steps. Teamsters were already clearing things out of the way. Heading back the way she'd been led, she saw a sign for a toilet ahead, and decided to take a detour. Go into the after-party without any distractions.

She was invited to the after-party, wasn't she?

She turned down an empty corridor, one of its lights blinking on and off, and headed towards the toilets, smiling stupidly. Of course she was invited. This hadn't gone the way she'd hoped, but so what. She'd enjoy the afterglow of the performance and only later, much later, bother thinking about the next step. Hell, she was floating on air, did she even need to go home tomorrow? Now she'd got Natalie's attention, she realised, she could enjoy whatever time they had together here – maybe even use this connection to persuade Ki to open up. He had to be impressed with what she'd done – Natalie had just worn his top for the whole world to see.

Tova slowed down before reaching the toilet door. A familiar feeling tickled at the back of her neck. The sensation of someone watching her. Or saying something unseen. The shadows shifted on the wall ahead and she turned to look back. Just inside the half-light of the corridor stood the big, squared-off Obake man and his thin accomplice, nothing between them and her. No one in the corridor behind them.

"Oh fuck," Tova said under her breath, taking a step back.

The men moved towards her. The shell suit one raised a hand and said something. Tova drew in a breath to shout for help – and as she did the corridor shook with the chants and cheers of the crowd beyond. Natalie's final song was finishing, the whole stadium was in uproar, and all Tova's shout did was spark the two men into action.

Tova ran. Before she had any idea what she was doing, she was past the toilet and racing for a pair of double doors at the end of the hall. She slammed through and kept going, bass shaking the ground as the music kicked back in. She was outside, into the night air, a wide lot of black buses with a handful of Teamsters smoking ahead. She opened her mouth to shout for help, but a hand clamped on her arm and she was jolted still.

Tova spun, terrified, to the face of the thin man. Gaunt, serious and eyeing her like a stain that needed cleaning. She took another breath to scream –

The sound caught in her throat as something hard pressed into her ribs, the man shifting closer to her. The barrel of a gun.

19

Tova trembled in the back of the car, windows too dark for anyone outside to see in.

They hadn't tied her, gagged her or anything like that. Nothing overt in the way they'd moved her, nothing to give anyone a clue that these two vile men were abducting her. The thin one had simply walked her out, unnoticed by the workers, and they'd waited on the road while the one in denim pulled the car round. She was shoved in and her captor followed, contact never waning. Only once they were driving did Tova's mind start racing with regrets – she should have screamed anyway; she should have run for the stage, screamed with everyone watching – they couldn't just shoot her. Should've done something better than ending up here.

Neither man addressed her or each other, that she saw. They sat stiffly as the car took her through the bright lights of central Tokyo. The gun rested casually on the thin man's lap, his stiff fingers occasionally twitching with suppressed aggression.

"What's going on?" Tova asked, muffling her own voice. If they assumed her to be deaf and dumb, as people did, maybe they'd take pity.

The thin man said something, tight lips barely moving. The big one, driving, gave her a look in the rear-view mirror. Still pissed at getting shocked by Ki?

Tova's eyes ran back to the gun. She had never seen one in real life, and it was a black, unfeeling object. If there was any possibility of her taking it, the man wouldn't have left it in reach. Perhaps he wanted her to try, to give himself a challenge, or to justify shooting her.

Someone would come, surely? Natalie Reid would realise Tova had disappeared. She'd know Tova wouldn't just leave, she'd do something. Or Ki – despite his deceptions, he would want a debrief, surely. He'd saved her before, he'd help her again.

The lights outside were getting dimmer, less frequent. Brilliant neon replaced by unlit, fettered banners and lanterns. On their way to a secluded execution ground...you foolish girl, you heard too much, no one must know that the city screams...

Sean Tasker, he'd know she was missing, he'd look for her, wouldn't he? Sure, in a week or two. Why hadn't she called him? Opened up about everything. He could've protected her, couldn't he? Why did she trust that manipulative little tailor over him?

Tova screwed her eyes closed. This couldn't be happening. Why her. Why now.

The thin man's jaw moved, saying something disapproving.

The driver's hand shifted to the radio, its screen lighting up as he turned a dial and changed the frequency. Tova's eyes stayed on it as he settled on a better station. She couldn't feel whatever they were listening to through the rumble of the car engine.

Tova's hand shifted towards a pocket. The VHR was in there, and for a moment she imagined a world where she could plug it in and make them hear the screams. Drive them to their knees, freeze them as all those people had frozen in the market. Taking the pistol might get her shot, but if they could only hear what she had heard...as her fingers traced over the VHR, they found something else. The small air horn she had bought.

Would that be loud enough?

The car slowed. Tova twisted as they passed a metro sign, but they were continuing, turning down a dark road now, no streetlights, barely any windows lit. Tova moved her hand into the pocket and, in a flash, one of the thin man's hands closed on her wrist. He glared into her face with the deep lines of a waxen horror figure.

"No. Moves," he enunciated clearly.

Tova swallowed and nodded.

The thin man pushed her hand out of the way and reached into the pocket himself. She cringed as he drew his hand out, and he regarded his find with a sneer. He'd taken the wrong object: the VHR. He looked at it without understanding and said something to the driver. The latter shrugged it off, not seeming to know nor care what it was. The thin man tossed it into the front seat.

The car turned another corner and continued between what looked like disused warehouses. The increasingly grimy structures reminded Tova finally of Ordshaw. Old industrial buildings left to ruin, the stomping grounds of criminals.

The thin man reached into his jacket, took out a piece of A4 paper and unfolded it. A single black and white photo, poor quality, of a Japanese man with a head of thick, curly hair, a disco afro. Somehow, Tova sensed at once who he was. Maybe it was the posture, the one hand adjusting the cuff of the other, or just his well-fitted suit. Ki. Young, immaculately dressed. It was low-resolution and the background was a blurred mess, some smear of light rising over his shoulders. A flapping cape?

The thin man thrust the picture towards Tova and made a demand. The big driver's hand flicked in front of her, clicking, and she pressed herself back into the seat. He was barking something, but with his clear anger and her own fearful state Tova couldn't read what. The thin man put up a calmer hand and his lips moved slowly, more clearly, "Where is he?"

And it clicked.

They didn't know what the VHR was, they didn't care about that, or whatever it might have done to Tova. They wanted Ki, not her. It had always been about him. They'd been in her building in Kabukicho before her not by some arcane means but because they were looking *for him*. And they'd come for her when...*fuck*, when she'd mentioned *Key Zero* online?

Tova shook her head, and said, "Don't understand."

"Understand this?" The thin man held up his pistol.

Tova resisted the urge to shake her head again.

The big guy thumped his hand into the steering wheel, lacking his colleague's patience. He barked something else, and the thin guy nodded.

"Foreign girl," the thin one said. His meaning was oddly clear, his broken English coming with careful pronunciation. He pointed at the picture, then at her. "He tells you lies? Help us, you go home safe. Yes?"

Tova swallowed. She said nothing, hoping they'd still take her for stupid. Even if she wanted to turn on Ki, even if there was a way she *could*, Tova didn't for a moment think these men would send her home. They had their hackles up already, wanted her blood.

"This" – the thin man held up the picture and jabbed at it with the pistol – "very dangerous man. He speak to you? Leave you notes?" He added one more question Tova didn't catch, and when she squinted he demonstrated with his free hand, covering his eyes. He repeated it and she got it: "You no saw him. No?"

Tova kept still, wishing for some kind of hint, finally, as to exactly who, or what, Ki was supposed to be.

"You lead us," the man demanded. "To him."

Tova stared blankly. She had to say something, even if there was nowhere she *could* lead them. Distract them long enough to roll out of the moving car. But she was frozen in fear, couldn't even produce a lie.

The thin man shook his head. "Phone? You have phone?"

Tova shrieked as he lunged at her, patting her pockets again. She hit her head on the car ceiling as she pushed away from him, but he ignored her reaction, reaching into another pocket. He took her phone and tapped at it, trying to get it to load. He thrust it at her to unlock it for him, gun pointing with the other hand, and she did so, quickly. She saw no new messages. No signal.

The thin man snatched it back and thumbed through with a look of distaste. He held it in her face, showing the messages from Ki, then snarled something at the driver. The big guy only seemed to get angrier. The thin one pocketed the phone and snarled his conclusions, saying *dangerous man* again. Something about the show, that they knew Tova had been sent there. They knew what Ki had been up to. Did they recognise his clothing?

"What he tell you?" The thin man turned another question on her. "Tell you of you say?"

Tova frowned, not sure she'd read that right. The man snapped something at the driver, who half-turned again and replied. They were talking Japanese, the words on their lips completely unclear – but Tova saw that same phrase again. A couple of times. Disagreeing about questioning her about it? It was the phrase the big one had said in the alley, before Ki shocked him. Not *you say* at all, but something in their own language.

Then that clicked, too. She'd looked up the word earlier that day. *Yōsei*. Did this mean she had got it right? This problem the men were taking very seriously, it was *fairies?*

"What he tell you?" The thin man was suddenly in her face, mouth stretched in a shout.

"Nothing!" Tova cried back.

The thin man shifted his grip on the pistol, ready to use it. He said something to the driver, then to Tova: "Time up."

Tova quickly shook her head. The dumb thing clearly wasn't

winning her sympathy, so she said, "I'll message him, set up a meeting – I can –"

He replied with a lopsided smile. "Know something, know nothing, no important."

"I know something," Tova said hurriedly. "Very important! Are you Obake Police? I –"

She cut herself off, the man's expression fixing on hearing the name. Tova understood two things in that moment: one, the Obake Police definitely existed, exactly as Ki had described them. Two, admitting that she knew that was a mistake.

There was no question in the man's face now, paired by the stiffening of the driver's shoulders. The thin man said something to the driver, swinging his gun around, and as the car started to pull over, Tova slammed her hand against her pocket, pressing the button of the air horn through the fabric.

The thin man threw his hands to his ears. The driver surged forwards in surprise and hit a pedal. Tova pressed down harder on the button, not letting it up as the car swerved. She rolled back in anticipation of the impact and was thrown into the driver's seat as the car crumpled into a wall. As they shook to a violent halt, she wrenched the horn out of her pocket and pressed it again, holding it up, closer to the thin man. Then she spun and shouldered into the door, pulling at the handle.

It didn't open. Locked. She turned back with terror.

The thin man was grimacing, face like a gargoyle as his eyes locked on her, hands still on his ears. He'd dropped the gun on the seat between them. They moved for it together, but as the man took a hand from his ear Tova jammed a finger onto the air horn again. It hit him like a punch and he flopped gracelessly forwards. Bucking into the door, Tova kicked at him, her heel catching his nose, before dragging the pistol her way. She fumbled it up into both hands, turning it towards the window, and twisted in the tight space as the man scrambled up her legs. As her finger hit the trigger she pulled it and the car lit up in a flash. The man's grasping hands fell back, showered with glass.

Tova gave the man a quick look. He was in agony from the air horn and the bang of the gunshot, mouth open in a wail. Worse than agony: blood trickled from his right ear. Tova spun to the window, cracked all around the top edge where the bullet went through, and she got her shoulder into it. A quick, sharp shove knocked it out, the remaining sheet of glass flopping onto the asphalt and shattering. She kicked and twisted her way through the frame, then fell heavily onto the tarmac. Tova rolled aside and scrambled backwards as she stood. The thin man launched at her, hands grabbing through the window, face livid. She was barely clear, but his fingers missed her, and she rapidly backpedaled. She lifted her hands, empty, the pistol dropped somewhere back near the car. But he was ungainly, much taller than her, having trouble navigating the small gap of the window. And the big driver beyond – he was just a shadow hulked over in the front. Motionless.

Panting her fear, Tova sprinted. As she reached the corner of the dark street she shot a look back: the thin man was oozing out of the window, trying to place his hands on the pavement somewhere between the shards of broken glass. He wasn't looking her way when she turned the corner. He wouldn't see which direction she went.

She sprinted on. There were lights ahead – a small alley of shops. She recognised the route they'd taken – kept running. Around another corner she spotted the metro sign. It took her into a department store, where she pushed through startled shoppers, snatching glances for more signs. She shoved through the ticket gates and vaulted down steps. A train had just pulled in, and she dived through the doors.

As it trundled out of the station she crouched by a window, looking back.

No sign of either man on the platform. She'd made it, surely?

Her heart was beating against her chest. She was totally out of breath. Everyone in the carriage was staring at her and she had no idea where she was going.

20

The airport was a bed of lights before a wide body of water, creeping dreamily into Tova's perception as she watched through the train window. She wasn't sure how she'd made sense of the metro map or how long she'd been travelling for, but apparently she'd made it. Fear and uncertainty, she realised, had brought her straight here and not to the British Embassy or anywhere else that she might find help. She was not sure there was anyone in this city she could trust. Even if there was, she'd only put them in terrible danger. She couldn't go back to the hotel, set up by Ki and Mei, which meant leaving behind her wardrobe and her Samsung tablet – her only means to contact home, now that she'd lost her phone. She couldn't go back into the city, to drag anyone else into those men's crosshairs. And there'd be no sense trying to get back to Natalie Reid; even if she could find her before the star retired to a lavish hotel or whatever else, the Obake Police would be watching her. So this was the plan Tova's subconscious had taken charge of: wait in the airport for her flight – half a day away – with her head down. Surprise everyone back home, after what would be a day of serious fretting.

The few people in the airport moved in the slow motion of a reluctant limbo, no one travelling so late by choice. Tova fit right in, dragging her feet towards a counter to check her tickets were valid. She asked them to scan the fake passport, too. The attendant at the counter, an ageless Japanese woman who could've been her hotel concierge's double, confirmed everything was in order, but pouted sympathy that Tova was here so early. She spoke at length – suggesting somewhere to go to while away the time, probably – and Tova didn't bother explaining she couldn't hear any of it. She wandered off to lie across a row of plastic chairs.

The VHR-38 was gone, she reflected. With that, she hoped, her connection to the screams of this city would be severed. Tokyo could keep them: better that no one know they exist, there was no way they pointed anywhere good. It was unnatural alright,

Mogami's insane research, and her surgery, and all things considered she'd been lucky to come out of this unscathed. Well, besides the cuts and scratches peppering her face and forearms from her smashed-window escape. She smirked. Together with the shaved patch on her head and the stains and tears her loud coat had endured, she was quite a sight. A survivor.

And as for the fairies. This idea of fairies existed, in whatever form they took. Dangerous people wanted to suppress them. Tokyo could keep that too, she decided.

Relaxing from her fears, telling herself it was over, Tova's eyelids drooped. She snapped herself awake a couple of times, catching moments of sleep. Then her eyes shot wide open when the shape of a man filled her vision.

Tova bolted upright, pressing herself back into the seat. They'd found her – they could find her anywhere –

Sean Tasker held up a hand for calm, saying something. He had another man with him, an older guy, tired and bald up top, suit much tattier. They had her pink suitcase standing between them, looking especially childish with its handle in Tasker's grip. Tova met each of their eyes in frightened turn, as Tasker attempted a friendly smile. When he spoke again, his companion translated it into British Sign Language.

"I thought you might want your luggage. We should talk, Tova."

Tova found herself in an exclusive waiting area, a sky lounge with low armchairs and colonial fixings, dark wood panelling and a chandelier yellowed by age. A uniformed concierge offered them tea; she said no, but Tasker ordered some anyway. He spoke without seeming to care that she couldn't hear him, and the translator appeared uncertain as to what to translate. Tova didn't catch the little that was signed, too busy studying Tasker's face. Had she escaped one execution to face another? They had tracked her to the hotel, and here, but they were alone, not flanked by any form of Japanese police – why?

When the tea arrived, Tasker's smile for the concierge came and went in an instant. He squeezed out the teabag, poured a cup for himself and one for Tova, then relaxed into his chair. She read his lips saying, "You've had quite a trip, I understand."

Tova nodded slowly.

"Quite an evening." The translator moved automatically at his side, but Tova got the message clearly enough. "Want to tell me about it?"

Tova said nothing, so he sipped at the tea. He made a comment about the quality, a connoisseur, then continued, "You should have stayed in the hospital. I could've protected you." He paused so Tova could give him a questioning look. "But you had other help eluding those men. The same help this evening?"

Tova shook her head. One thing was sure in her mind: she'd been left to hang by Ki.

Tasker's eyes ran over her face, to the barely dried cuts on her hands. As he spoke, the translator signed, "You're not in any trouble. The Japanese police would like to ask you some questions, but we don't believe it's necessary. We think it's best they don't know where you are."

It was a strange start, but a good one. If she could play these two sides against each other, she was all for that. She said, "They had a gun. They wanted to hurt me."

Tasker registered no surprise. "Well, they won't find you now. I caught up to Natalie Reid's people before they did, and we've kept your assumed name safe." Her government had spoken to Natalie about her? They knew about the passport, presumably, too? Tova tried to keep one eye on Tasker, one on the translator. "Until you're out of Japan, I feel it's our duty, for the safety of a British citizen, to look the other way. But the more you talk to me the better I can resolve this misunderstanding with the locals."

Misunderstanding? In the same breath he admitted she needed a fake identity to leave the country, he was suggesting the Japanese could be calmed with an amiable chat? She said, "They were going to kill me."

He responded with a half-smile of confirmation. "Two of their men are badly injured, so let's say we're even."

Like the Obake's ill-intentions were balanced by their failure. That absurdity, Tova realised, only spoke to how serious this was. Threats against life, given to flippant negotiation. She said, "They still want me, though?"

Tasker turned his appeasing smile to the translator now, who didn't look like he wanted to be there. Not just because it was late. Tova watched the signing as Tasker spoke. "Give it time, they'll lose interest. It's important we get an understanding of exactly what you went through, though."

"To decide how much trouble I'm in?" Tova answered, warily. Home was within reach, and Tasker was at least pretending to be reasonable: she just had to convince him she knew nothing worth their time. "I don't know what this is even about. I started hearing things, everyone said it was in my head, why is it an international incident?"

"These Japanese guys," Tasker said, "did they say anything to you?"

Tova hesitated. There was no sense in claiming complete ignorance, and it wasn't as if she could give Ki up, anyway. Still, she felt concerned about revealing too much. Like the Obake, Tasker had to have particular reasons for being here, which she needed to stay disconnected from. "They asked about a man, I understood that. Only that, really. But I never met him. I don't know who he is or what he did. I did speak to him, though. I mean, he messaged me. He said he wasn't allowed near Natalie Reid, but wanted me to give her a gift. I thought it was weird but why not? I wanted to make a good impression..."

"The t-shirt, that was the gift?" Tasker asked.

Tova nodded. "I know it was stupid – now – it could've been anything. A bomb, poison. Was it dangerous?"

"I doubt it. Did he give you anything else?"

She quickly shook her head.

"But you knew he was trouble. You relocated, you left the hospital –"

"Yes. Well." Tova stirred a foot. "He offered me an upgrade, in exchange for helping him. It was strange, definitely strange, but did you see where I was staying? I was careful, I told my parents back home, they contacted the embassy."

Tasker offered his smile again. "How did he communicate with you?"

"Passed a letter under the door, in Kabukicho," Tova lied. "He wrote his phone number and we exchanged texts. I'd show you but I lost my phone. He warned me these people were watching the hospital because I was in touch with him." Tova paused as those words came out, realising that was actually true. Had his presence stopped her from getting more help? Was anyone really interested in suppressing the effects of her hearing operation? No, she had to keep firm. That problem, the one that was uniquely hers, was still connected to Ki's technology, and that made it dangerous. She said, "Who *is* this guy?"

"Did he give you a name?"

"Ki."

"Nothing more?"

Tova nodded.

Another moment passed, Tasker thinking. At last, Tasker said, "A rare mistake, apparently – it's likely that's how they connected you to him." Ki said it was a common name. The *zero*, presumably, was the identifying part. But if Tasker knew that, it didn't seem important, as he continued. Tova watched the interpreter sign: *What else did you talk about? What did he tell you?*

"Not much," Tova said. "He gave me recommendations for local places to visit. He said people were after him, but never why. Was it something to do with my operation?" She let that hang there. The big question, considering Tasker had come via the hospital.

"Do you have reason to believe it was?" Tasker turned the question back to her. His posture shifted, one shoulder tilted forwards. Danger, danger: hadn't Eguchi disappeared when he showed up? Secret Agent Man: on hand to check you don't know anything you shouldn't. The men in the car made their minds up the instant Tova used the word Obake. Revealing what her ear surgery had exposed her to was not going to win her friends.

She shook her head. "What has Ki done? Did I put Natalie Reid in danger?"

Tasker's humourless smile held a slight tinge of sympathy. "You don't have any idea? Didn't see or hear anything else strange?"

"I didn't see anything. And I *can't* hear."

Tasker's smile twisted awkwardly. "But you reported these screams –"

"Which I imagined, right? Dr Eguchi wouldn't even see me when I came back, they thought I was wasting their time. Do you know something else? Is it possible I didn't imagine it?"

The smile was gone. "Have you heard them again?" She'd gone too far, hit back on the truth, and he was trying to draw it out of her. Definitely something in it, but if it was safe to know, to ask, why wasn't he offering an explanation?

"It's over, isn't it?" Tova said. "There were no screams, the operation was a complete failure. They messed me up, that's all. My life savings got me sounds in my head and the attention of some weirdo stalker." She put on her most innocent look. "I just want to go home."

Her plight appeared to have no effect on the agent; he simply stared, cold and hard.

Tova added, "I didn't see anything. I didn't really hear anything, did I? I wanted to..."

Tasker still didn't respond, and the translator at his side shifted uncomfortably, feeling bad for her. Tasker moved a hand to the pink bag near the table, found the handle without taking his eyes off Tova. She longed for it back, to have her tablet, to message home. He offered one last couple of questions, something to do with *anything else* she wanted to add.

Tova held off for a second, looking aside to suggest thinking. She shook her head. Tasker considered it for a moment, then pushed her bag closer to her, stood and buttoned his jacket, taut over his chest. The translator stood too, flitting relieved glances between him and Tova. Tasker's crocodile smile returned. "I'm sorry for all you've been through." Tova studied his lips, snapping her attention briefly to the translator's signing so she didn't miss a word. "My colleagues in Ordshaw might be in touch. And we'll make sure Mogami follow up with you. It's unacceptable, what they put you through."

Tova held her breath as Tasker stalled, raising a thoughtful finger.

"How was it, meeting Natalie Reid?" His smile finally seemed genuine, actually curious. "I've seen interviews. Special woman, that one, isn't she?"

Tova managed to smile herself, the one good memory she could take from all this. "She was nice. I really liked her."

"You talked to her, about all this? What you'd been through, where the top came from?"

Tova shook her head. "I didn't say much. She's so busy..."

"I bet that was something," Tasker continued. "Natalie Reid, I got a daughter that'd kill to meet her." The translator's hands moved hesitantly as Tova got the gist from Tasker's amused lips. "Honest to God, claw her own face off to get a ticket. You're both from Ordshaw? You talk about that? Special city, too."

There was that word again. Special woman, special city. He

was still trying to draw her out. Tova cleared her throat, and said, "Will Natalie be in trouble, because of me?"

"Oh no," Tasker said. "No one's going to kick up a fuss over a t-shirt. Look, I couldn't say exactly what the Japanese want with your friend, but you got caught in a small part of something bigger. Hopefully you'll never hear from him again." He paused, then concluded, "Have a good life, Tova."

With that, he marched away, straight-backed, done. The translator took a moment to sign farewell before rushing after him. Tova half rose from her chair, watching as the men left, neither talking. Then the room was empty bar herself and the waiter stacking teacups on the bar. Tova slid back down into the seat, scarcely daring to blink in case she jinxed this moment. That was it? She was free to go? Free to use a fake passport to leave the country, defying the local police?

But of course they'd believed her. A simple deaf girl, caught up in their intrigue, what could she possibly know? Tova sat motionless, letting that soak in. What *did* she know? From the way Tasker had spoken, she knew more than she should but much less than the whole. With that weighing on her, pressing her down into the armchair, she let exhaustion take over. She was finally free, anyway, now, wasn't she?

When Tova woke, she hurried wearily out of the sky lounge, fighting the urge to collapse again lest she miss her flight. She checked in and dragged herself around the departure lounge on automatic. After breakfast in a café – a fishy sticky rice dish, one last oddity – and a few final quirky shops, she tiredly stood in queue for the flight. Could've jumped to the front citing disability, but why bother. She could handle a lot more than queuing.

While she waited, she scanned the people around her, many of them Westerners, on their way back to Ordshaw. Had any of them had a journey as wild as hers? This portly man in a blazer might've been visiting a secret family. That pair of middle-aged women wearing sunglasses, on this grey day, had they both endured a hedonistic bender, unclear which memories of garish lighting were real and which were hallucinations?

Tova ambled onto the plane and nestled into her seat, then turned her attention away from the other passengers to out the window, taking in the skyline. They might've had secrets, and parties, and thrills, but quite definitely, no one had experienced the same city as her. Tokyo was screaming, and this *yōsei* technology had connected her to that. There were *fiends* out there that no one but she had heard. The only people she could safely share that with were more interested in promoting clothing, so the secret sat on her shoulders alone. She could outrun it, but it wasn't going away. Mei had said her people were also in Ordshaw. Tasker had come probing for a reason. While this city was screaming, what was going on unseen back home?

As the plane took off, Tova watched the mountains of Tokyo's towers getting smaller and picked out a familiar building. The Tokyo Dome, its white roof breaking up the metropolis like a vast air balloon. She had been there, on the stage, with everyone cheering Natalie Reid. With Natalie cheering *her*. As Tova soared higher, the city shrank beneath her. And she smiled, picturing those countless happy people screaming in joy instead of fear.

ENJOYED READING?

If you enjoyed *The City Screams*, there's plenty more at large in the world of Ordshaw. The main series opens with *Under Ordshaw*, itself part of a three-book arc exploring exactly what lies beneath Tova's home city. It's not Tova's tale, yet, but she will return. Look out for the next in the series soon.

To be the first to hear news of the upcoming books, and for some free reads and other great offers, join my mailing list; you can find it via the various web addresses below.

And while you're waiting for more, I have a request myself: it would make a huge difference if you could leave a review of this book online (even just a few words helps). As an independent author, I rely on fans like you to let others know my books are worth reading!

ABOUT THE AUTHOR

Phil Williams is the author of the Estalia, Ordshaw and Faergrowe series. Living in Sussex, UK, with his wife, he also writes screenplays and spends a great deal of time walking his impossibly fluffy dog, Herbert.

www.phil-williams.co.uk

You can also connect with Phil through:
Facebook: **www.facebook.com/philwilliamsauthor**
Twitter: **www.twitter.com/fantasticphil**
Email: **phil@phil-williams.co.uk**

A NOTE FROM THE AUTHOR

The City Screams is an unusual book, primarily because it was originally conceived as a short story. Combining elements from an idea that emerged during writing *Blue Angel* with an unpublished sci-fi short I wrote a few years back, I saw an opportunity to explore a thread of the Ordshaw saga otherwise scheduled many, many books down the line. The lynchpin, which also made the whole affair so complicated, was the emergence of Tova.

Deafness is a topic I first took a real interest in whilst raising funding for an app aimed at connecting disability communities. During my research into disabilities I was fascinated to learn about the Deaf community, and the idea that the world could be seen so differently through others' eyes. I have many people to thank for educating me in this, most particularly John Walker, of Sussex University, who kindly met with me back then and helped me find feedback for this project, years later. In turn, John led me to lecturer Dai O'Brien, who gave me some excellent advice on this book, at a time when I was struggling to find Deaf SFF fants to help (and I wouldn't have dreamed of releasing such a book without at least *some* feedback). I'd also like to thank Mark Schofield and Vanessa Wells for their supportive emails during my search.

As always, my immense thanks goes out to my editor Carrie O'Grady, who did another fine job with the polish, and to my wife, Marta, whose enthusiasm to visit Japan probably played a part in the festering emergence of this book's setup.

ALSO BY PHIL WILLIAMS

The *Ordshaw* Series

UNDER ORDSHAW
There's something lurking under her city.
Knowing it's there could get her killed.
Pax is one rent cheque away from the unforgiving streets of Ordshaw. After her stash is stolen, her hunt for the thief unearths a book of nightmares and a string of killers, and she stands to lose much more than her home.
Can she decipher the mysteries of the Sunken City, before they consume her?

BLUE ANGEL
THE VIOLENT FAE

The *Estalia* Series

WIXON'S DAY
BALFAIR'S CONFINEMENT
AFTAN WHISPERS

The *Faergrowe* Series

A MOST APOCALYPIC CHRISTMAS

www.ingramcontent.com/pod-product-compliance
Lightning Source LLC
Chambersburg PA
CBHW021023120726
47905CB00009B/3152